Irresistible

Greg watched Katie's face as she talked — it made him feel warm and happy just to look at her. Although it wasn't right to sit there and have feelings like this for another guy's girl friend, Greg hadn't felt like this since . . . since he'd first met Chris.

They stopped talking and just sat looking at each other. Greg couldn't resist leaning closer to Katie. He put one hand on the back of her neck and brought his face close to hers. When he began to kiss her, she responded warmly. The longer he held her, the more passion he felt flowing through them.

Books from Scholastic in the **Couples** series:

HEAD OVER HEELS

M.E. Cooper

SCHOLASTIC INC.
New York Toronto London Auckland Sydney

ISBN 0-590-40796-1

12 11 10 9 8 7 6 5 4 3 2 1   7 8 9/8 0 1 2/9

Printed in the U.S.A.   01

First Scholastic printing, October 1987

Chapter
1

Katie Crawford took a deep breath and let it out with a *whoosh*. Only fifteen more double leg lifts to go. She turned her head and looked wistfully out the open window of Kennedy High's weight room. Outside the sun was bright and the air was balmy — a perfect fall day. She *could* be roller-skating in Rosemont Park instead of steaming away in here. But gymnastics season, her last one at Kennedy, was only a few months away. It was important to stay in the best shape possible. So here she was, doing Nautilus on this gorgeous October afternoon. She sighed and lifted her legs once more.

Just then, Katie's favorite song from the live Springsteen album came blaring out of her portable tape player. She started singing along as well as she could, considering she was breathless from her workout. It's a good thing I have the place to myself, she thought wryly. She knew she must be quite a sight, with her auburn bangs plastered to her forehead and her bare knees poking from the holes in her oldest pair of exercise tights. Not to mention quite a sound! She loved to sing, but she wasn't exactly glee club material.

The Kennedy weight room was a nice change from the Fitness Center downtown where she usually worked out with her gymnastics coach, Mr. Romanski. The equipment there was fancier but the gym was often mobbed. Later in the day the Kennedy weight room would be overrun by athletes coming in from soccer, football, and field hockey practice, but right now it was as private as the workout area in Katie's own basement at home.

Katie put all her might into her last leg lift. Her muscles burned, just as they should. The moment she and Bruce finished their song in a rising crescendo, a deep voice behind her said, "Hey, can I have your autograph?"

Katie tipped her head back and looked straight into the blue-green eyes of Greg Montgomery. They both burst out laughing.

"Oh, it's only you!" Greg pretended to be surprised. "For a minute there I thought it was the Boss himself, pumping iron in our very own gym. But now that I take a closer look" — he ran his eyes over her and smiled — "there's no mistaking the fantastic shape of star gymnast Katie Crawford!"

Katie blushed despite herself as she sat up and grabbed her towel from the windowsill. She snapped it playfully at Greg, then wiped her forehead. "You're too much, Monty!"

Once she was sitting up, she could take a good look at the boy who had joined her in the weight room. Greg's broad, tanned chest was bare, and a turquoise T-shirt was slung over one muscular shoulder. His sandy hair was damp at the temples. When Katie hopped down and stood next to him, she didn't even come up to his shoulders.

"What have you been doing? Running a marathon?" she asked, tipping her head so that her thick red ponytail bounced. Katie couldn't help noticing that he looked fantastic.

"Running laps on the track outside," he answered. "I've been a little lazy lately, but it's time to start pushing myself. Crew starts this weekend; we're rowing against Leesburg and Hinsdale on Saturday." He flexed one arm and grimaced at Katie. "Think I need a miracle to get this body ready in twenty-four hours?"

Katie pretended to consider his question seriously. "Well," she said, narrowing her eyes. "Maybe not a *miracle*. Maybe just a thousand more laps and about a million sit-ups and — "

Greg waved a hand at her and grinned. "Okay, okay! I get the picture."

Katie settled herself at the next machine. Time to work on her back and shoulders. She was still watching Greg out of the corner of her eye as he added a few extra pounds to the free weights. She knew him slightly; he was a junior and they were part of the same extended crowd at Kennedy. Just last spring they were both involved in an athletics funding dispute at school. As a matter of fact, that was how Katie had met her boyfriend,

Eric Shriver, who was captain of the boys' swim team.

Katie remembered how angry Greg had been when his girl friend, Chris Austin, the student body president, had had responsibility for evaluating the financial needs of all of Kennedy's teams and making recommendations about funding to the school board. She had cut back the already paltry support Greg's brand-new crew team received. Katie had gotten the impression that, in her effort not to be partial to Greg's team, Chris had bent over backward in the opposite direction. It had all worked out in the end, though. Greg refused to give up and had gone out fundraising on his own. Katie had really admired his drive and dedication. As a result, the crew team was still afloat — no pun intended, she thought to herself mischievously.

Girls' gymnastics, meanwhile, had gotten its fair share. After their strong season last winter, with Katie leading the way into the state finals, she expected more support from both the fans *and* the school board this year.

At the moment gymnastics was about the furthest thing from Katie's mind. She was too busy absorbing the fact that Greg Montgomery was absolutely gorgeous. She had always known he was handsome and charismatic. That was no secret to any girl at Kennedy. But she'd never been alone with him before. In these close quarters, he was even more impressive. Katie found herself wondering how she looked — whether her hair was a total mess and if her old, baggy leotard flattered her slim figure or made her look frumpy.

She was so lost in thought that she didn't notice Greg had put down the weights and was watching her quietly. He broke into her reverie by sending her a smile so warm and electric that she jumped.

She met his glance squarely and smiled back. "What are you looking at?" She looked down ruefully at her ragged knees. "My fancy tights?"

Greg shook his head. "No, I was just admiring your technique. You really know how to work out."

Katie raised an eyebrow. "I bet you say that to all the girls!"

He grinned. "Nope. I'm pretty sure that's the first time I've used that particular line! Anyway, I mean it!"

"Thanks."

He started lifting again. "What are you doing in here, anyway? Isn't gymnastics a winter sport?"

"Yeah." Katie paused to adjust her leotard, which was slipping off one shoulder. "But you know how it is. I have to train year-round. I've hardly missed a day since I was six years old!" She laughed. "I knew that was the only way to become really good, and that's what I wanted more than anything."

"Well, it sure looks like it paid off! I've only seen you perform once — last year at the state finals, when you blew away all the competition," Greg said, impressed. "But this year I'll be sure to reserve front row seats at every meet. Or should I be planning to watch you at the Olympics?"

"No way. Mary Lou Retton I'm not and never will be!" Katie shrugged and smiled. "But that's okay. Competing at the high school level is enough for me. I just love the sport, you know?"

Greg put away the free weights and then paused at the rowing machine. His eyes met hers and the light in them told Katie he understood exactly how she felt. "I really will be there to watch you. Front and center."

Katie felt a warm glow inside her that wasn't just from strenuous exercise. She could tell Greg meant what he said. It always gave her a boost when a friend was in the audience at a meet. Her best friend, Molly Ramirez, had been a regular last winter, but Eric had always been too busy with his own swim meets to watch her. That had been a big disappointment for Katie early in their relationship. Now she pictured herself earning a perfect ten on the balance beam with Greg Montgomery cheering her on. She was surprised by how good that thought made her feel.

"Did I hear that you have a crew meet tomorrow?" she asked. "I thought you rowed in the spring."

"We do," he answered, settling onto the rowing machine and taking a powerful stroke. Katie tried not to stare at the muscles bunching and unbunching on his bare back and shoulders. "There's a longer, more intense season in the spring but most schools have a fall season, too. I got Kennedy into some of the races. We could use the extra edge this practice will give us."

"That's great! It's a good excuse to be outside in weather like this, anyway." Although, she added to herself, for the past fifteen minutes I haven't minded being inside at all!

Greg nodded, and when he spoke his voice was enthusiastic. "I love rowing in the fall. It's even better than summer — the sun is still warm, but the air is really sharp and clean. It makes you want to fly. I bet you'd like it, too."

Katie wrinkled her nose doubtfully. "I think I'll leave the water sports to Eric."

"C'mon, I thought you were the adventurous type!"

"Maybe, but I don't think I'd feel safe in one of those little boats — what do you call them — shells?" Katie giggled. "Give me the *Love Boat* any day!"

"I'm disappointed in you," Greg said in a sorrowful tone. "Giving up on what could be one of the great experiences of your life without even trying it once."

"Be fair!" Katie exclaimed. "I'd like to see *you* jump on the uneven bars and give it a whirl, just like that. I bet you'd have second thoughts."

He took another powerful stroke on the rowing machine and grinned broadly. "You've got me there. I'd be scared stiff."

After working out in silence for a few minutes, they both started talking at the same moment, then burst out laughing.

"What were you going to say?" Katie asked. She'd finished her Nautilus routine and was sitting on the mats, propped up by her elbows.

Greg had picked up a jump rope, but now he

dropped it in order to drop himself right on the mat beside her. "You first," he said, wiping his forehead with the back of his hand. He looked at her expectantly.

Katie gulped. She wasn't about to admit that by sitting so close to her Greg had driven every intelligent thought from her head. She started doing sit-ups to cover her confusion.

"Um, so . . . what did you think about the homecoming football game?" she finally managed to ask. She made a wry face to herself as she pulled her left knee up to meet her chin. Oh, boy. What a way to start an exciting conversation!

Greg joined her doing sit-ups. "It was great — it's always a riot losing to Leesburg."

Katie laughed. It was the first time in years that Kennedy had lost a homecoming game. "I don't remember seeing you there, though," she added. Then she was struck by a thought. Had Chris Austin, who was now a freshman at Mount Holyoke College, come home for the weekend? A lot of recent Kennedy grads did. Katie was suddenly very curious about the state of affairs between Greg and Chris. She thought they'd broken up, but she wasn't sure.

Katie figured there couldn't be any harm in asking — in a roundabout way. "Did Chris come home from college for the game?" She tried to sound nonchalant.

"No, she didn't." Greg's voice, aside from a slight grunt as he completed a sit up, was casual. Not too much hidden emotion there, Katie decided.

"I guess she's having a good time at school," he continued. "Anyway, she had just been home for a visit a couple of weeks before homecoming." He laughed and then groaned. "Katie, do I have to keep up with you sit-up for sit-up? You're cruel."

Greg was breathing hard, but Katie just laughed. She could tell he wasn't making as much of an effort as he pretended. He was obviously in excellent shape — a guy didn't get a body like that from sitting around watching TV.

"Like I was saying," he went on, "Chris has her own life now." He gritted his teeth. "And I have *my* own life. I'm actually having a lot of fun without her." He smiled at Katie and she knew he must be referring to his brief romance with Kirsten Berg, one of the three beautiful Swedish exchange students who had recently taken Kennedy High by storm.

"Yeah, in a situation like that I guess you really do have to be independent," Katie agreed. "I mean, it's always important to do your own thing." Her stomach muscles were burning, but she was too interested in her conversation with Greg to stop. "Have you heard from Kirsten lately?"

"We've written back and forth a couple of times. I'm not sure how long it will last, though. There's not much point."

Katie hesitated. "No, I guess not." She had a hard time imagining what it must be like for Greg to deal with two relationships that ended in long distance separation. Eric was her first boyfriend and neither of them was going anywhere.

If they were, with graduation coming up in the spring, they were going there together.

Suddenly Katie paused halfway through a sit-up and clutched her stomach. She turned to Greg, panting and laughing. "*What* are we doing?! Going for a world record?"

Greg fell on his back, his arms flung wide. "You've killed me!" he yelped. "I'll never sit up again!"

Katie collapsed next to him giggling helplessly. "I'm sorry! I don't know what came over me."

She turned her flushed face toward Greg. He was as red as she was. His ham expression of exhausted agony only made her laugh harder. Then he put on a serious face.

"K.C.," he began, his voice deep and important. He was so close to her she could see the green flecks in his blue eyes. Her heart had been pounding double time, and now it just about stopped.

"Greg — " she responded in as serious a tone as she could muster.

Greg cut in smoothly. "I think there's only one way to recover from this workout."

Katie's eyes were still locked on his. "Only one?" she echoed weakly.

He nodded solemnly and then whispered, "A double chocolate milk shake at the sub shop."

Katie let out a whoop. "Let's go!"

Three minutes later, after throwing her sweats on over her leotard and lacing up her high tops, Katie was striding across the school parking lot under the bright blue autumn sky with Greg.

They were still talking as she unlocked her mom's red Plymouth Voyager — and as they drove around the crowded parking lot in front of the sub shop looking for a space, and as they settled into a booth in the back after waving hello to Elise Hammond and Emily Stevens.

They were still talking when they left the sub shop an hour later, both surprised to find that the afternoon had passed and it was already getting dark. When Katie shivered in the now-cool air, Greg put an arm around her shoulders. He gave her a quick friendly squeeze.

"Want to wear my jacket until you get home?" he asked solicitously.

"I'll be all right," Katie assured him. She buckled her seat belt and turned the key in the ignition, then realized she didn't even know where Greg lived. "Where am I taking you, anyway?" she asked, flipping on the headlights.

"Cliffside Avenue. You know how to get there from here, right?" Greg paused for a moment, then added, "Listen, Katie. There's something I've been wanting to ask you all afternoon."

Oh, my gosh, he's going to ask me on a date, Katie thought suddenly, her eyes widening. She noticed that Greg had put his hand on the back of her seat and it gave her goosebumps. Doesn't he know I have a boyfriend? What am I going to say?

"It's about crew," he continued brightly. It was all Katie could do to keep from laughing out loud. "I really do wish you'd think about trying out. I mean, you're too small to row, but you're just the right size for a coxswain."

Katie shot him a skeptical glance as she turned on to Cliffside Avenue. "Me?"

"Yes, you! You'd be great. I just have this feeling about it." His eyes crinkled as he smiled. "I'm not kidding, K.C. This is a serious proposition! My best cox graduated last year, and I've been training someone new but it's not working out too well." Katie kept her eyes glued to the road, but she could feel Greg leaning toward her. "So what do you say? Will you give it a try? That is, if you think you could handle being alone in a small boat with eight big, strong males."

Katie laughed. "Sounds like fun to me! I tell you what, I'll think about it. I mean, I wouldn't want it to interfere with my gymnastics season."

"Then I guess I'll have to settle for that. This is it." Greg waved a hand at the next driveway on the left, and Katie pulled over to the curb. She caught a glimpse of a large brick house beyond a thick wall of rhododendrons.

"Would you like to come up for a while?" Greg asked. "It's always cocktail hour around now at the Montgomery's."

"No, I really should be getting home," Katie said regretfully. "It's always help-Mom-with-dinner hour around now at the Crawfords. But thanks, anyway."

He laughed. "Okay. Well, thanks for the ride." He put a hand on the door handle and then turned back to her. He held her eyes for a long moment before he spoke again, and Katie couldn't help recalling the impression she'd gotten that afternoon — that since Chris had gone to college, Greg was ready for something new. She put her hands on her knees and gripped them tightly. She wasn't sure what it was she saw in Greg's eyes; she only knew she couldn't look away.

"And thanks for a wonderful afternoon," he added, his voice soft. Then he grinned. "I never thought I could have such a good time lifting weights!"

Katie brushed back her bangs and laughed. "Me, either," she said sincerely. "See ya."

"See ya," Greg echoed as he climbed out of the car. "Maybe tomorrow at the crew race?"

"Maybe!" Katie waved good-bye and shifted into first. She drove home, oblivious to the brilliant October sunset. She was too busy thinking about Greg and sit-ups and chocolate milk shakes and crew to register much of anything else.

She parked in the driveway of her family's house on Magnolia Street, grabbed her duffel bag, and raced inside. As usual this time of day, her mother was leaning over a large saucepan on the stove and, as usual, her two younger brothers were watching some annoying rerun on TV in the den.

Mrs. Crawford gave her daughter a welcoming smile. "Hi, Katie. How was your day?"

"Great, Mom. Busy! I went to the sub shop after the gym — that's why I'm so late. I'll be down to help you in a minute. I'm just going to jump in the shower first."

Katie took the stairs three at a time. She yanked the green and white checkered curtains in her bedroom closed before stripping off her sweats, leotard, and tights.

As she took the elastic band off her ponytail

and shook out her thick red hair, she realized she was still thinking about Greg. Well, that's natural, she told herself. I just spent a few hours with him. She wrapped her blue plaid flannel bathrobe around her and belted it snugly. Not only that, she thought, but they were a few really *fun* hours. In fact, she hadn't enjoyed talking to anyone so much in a long time.

She padded down the hall to the bathroom and turned on the shower, hopping up and down in her bare feet on the cold tile floor while she waited for the water to heat up. She suddenly felt very disloyal to Eric. Of course she loved talking to him, too. Sure, they mostly talked about ordinary everyday things, but that was just because they talked so often they *had* to talk about that sort of stuff.

But even as she was mentally defending Eric, Katie couldn't deny to herself that Greg had really made an impression on her. Now that she was home with her feet firmly planted on the floor of the bath tub, she was almost amazed at just how much of an impression he had made. A couple of times with him that afternoon she'd felt sort of like she had before she started seeing Eric — when she didn't have a boyfriend and had a crush on someone.

How strange, Katie thought as she worked up a lather in her hair. Why would Greg, or anyone for that matter, have that kind of effect on me when I'm perfectly happy with Eric? She didn't have an answer.

She rinsed her hair and hurried through the rest of her shower. All she wanted to do now was

14

call Eric and hear his voice. They were supposed to go to a movie tonight — she'd tell him how much she was looking forward to it. And she *was* looking forward to it. There was no one in the world she'd rather be with. She'd be crazy to let another guy turn her head.

Katie plugged in her blow dryer and then faced the mirror. She closed her eyes for a second and pictured herself at the movies . . . with Greg.

She shook her head and turned on the dryer, staring at her reflection in the mirror. She didn't want to admit to herself that for the first time in the six months she and Eric had been going out, there was another guy on her mind. Although maybe that wasn't necessarily a bad thing. She decided — she hoped — an evening with Eric would put Greg back where he belonged, in the background of her life.

Chapter
2

Katie was halfway down the stairs when the doorbell rang. She stopped for a second in the hall to adjust one of the stirrups on her new black leggings. It was just eight o'clock. Her bracelets jingled as she swung the front door open.

"Hey, Katie!"

"Hi, Eric!"

Katie felt her face break into a big warm smile like the one she saw on Eric's face. This always happened to her when she saw him, even if they'd only separated a few minutes before. Tonight Eric had her beaming like a lighthouse. Of course nothing had changed just because she had a good time at the gym with Greg Montgomery. What had she been so worried about?

Katie was still mentally shaking her head at her own foolishness as she and Eric called out good-night to her parents and headed for his Mustang. Before they climbed into the car, he wrapped his arms around her waist and easily picked her up and swung her around. Katie shrieked and giggled, beating playfully at his shoulders.

"Put me down, you beast!"

Eric gave her one last twirl and then deposited her gently on the curb. "Just shaking you up a little!" he declared. "You seem kind of spacy."

"Well, I'm wide awake now, thank you very much!"

He opened the door for her. She settled in the passenger seat and then leaned over to push his door open. Once he was inside he turned to smile at her, the dimple in his right cheek deepening. Katie smiled back.

As if reading her mind, Eric touched a finger to her cheek. "I'm so happy when I'm with you, Katie," he said simply.

"I know what you mean," Katie said. She smiled and turned sideways in her seat so she could put her arms around his neck and twist her fingers through his wavy light brown hair. "Kind of like you just won a gold in the Olympics, huh? I feel that way every day when I think about you."

"You mean more to me than any medal ever could," Eric said. He pulled Katie close to him, then lowered his lips over hers for a long, sweet kiss. His arms were always strong and hard from swimming, and when they were around her Katie felt safe and warm and loved. It was a feeling she didn't think she'd ever get tired of.

Eric nuzzled her neck. "What do you say we go see a movie?"

17

"Oh, I don't know." Katie gave him a squeeze. "I'm kind of having fun right here, aren't you?"

Eric kissed her on the tip of the nose and peered out the car window. "Yeah, but don't you think your parents will notice if we never leave the driveway?"

She giggled. "Maybe you're right."

As they headed for the movie theater at the mall, Katie watched Eric out of the corner of her eye. His hair, his cute blond eyelashes, those amazingly green eyes, his dimples. . . . It was all still there, that same old chemical reaction. She held back a sigh of relief. I'm still in love with Eric! She wanted to shout out the car window. *Yahoo!*

Eric rolled down his own window a few inches and the smell of wet, earthy, fallen leaves filled the air. "How was your day, anyway? I missed you at lunch."

"I know, I ate my sandwich in the greenhouse," Katie explained. "The alfalfa sprouts Molly and I planted never sprouted, and we had to start our biology lab project over from scratch." She rolled her eyes. "Farmers we'll never be!"

Eric grinned. "Jonathan and I had trouble with that lab, too, but it was because *our* plants got to be *gigantic* — at least ten times bigger than everybody else's. That's when we realized we'd used tomato seeds instead of alfalfa!"

Katie hooted. "I bet you thought you'd invented some kind of monster sprout."

"Yeah, we could have gotten rich. Oh, well." He gripped the steering wheel with his left hand

and put his free arm around her, rubbing her shoulder through her loose jade green sweater. "Are you stiff, K.C.? Have a tough workout?"

Katie shrugged. For some reason she was glad that Eric's hand dropped from her shoulder. "Kind of." She studied his unconcerned profile. "Actually," she added, somewhat hesitantly, "it was a fun one. I ran into Greg Montgomery in the gym at school and we sort of had an accidental sit-up contest." She laughed at the recollection and Eric glanced at her. "Guess what? He asked me to try out for crew as a coxswain! Isn't that wild?"

Eric narrowed his eyes and looked in the rearview mirror. "What do you know about being a cox?"

"Well, nothing, but I could always learn." Katie was a little surprised at Eric's tone. It wasn't exactly delighted. "I mean, I didn't say I would. I might try, that's all."

"You don't have the time, though," he observed. "You're a one-sport girl."

Katie bristled slightly. Did he think she wouldn't be good at crew? Then she relaxed. There was no reason to get edgy. Eric didn't mean anything.

"I *do* have time, though. This is off season, remember? I can work on my gymnastics any time of the day or night until team practice starts in December."

Eric shook his head as he pulled into a parking space behind the theater. When he looked at her, his expression was still questioning. "But what about us?"

"What do you mean, what about us?" Katie asked, confused.

"I don't know." Eric turned off the engine and opened his door. He walked around to Katie's side and took her hand. He swung it as they walked across the parking lot together. "It just seems like we have little enough time for each other as it is." Before Katie could become too angry, Eric gave her an irresistible smile. "I guess I don't want to share you with anyone," he admitted, squeezing her hand. "Is that okay?"

Katie tingled right down to her toes. "Yeah, it is." She stood on tiptoes to kiss him on the cheek. "I think I like you feeling that way about me."

In the mall they argued playfully for five minutes about which of two movies to see and then decided on a third. They bought a large tub of popcorn dripping with butter and found seats in the back of the theater. As they were sitting down, Katie caught sight of a few familiar faces. Fiona Stone, Jonathan Preston, Fiona's brother Jeremy, and Diana Einerson were a few rows ahead of them. She and Eric tossed their jackets on the seats and strolled down the aisle to say hello.

"What's happening?" Eric greeted the others. He high-fived Jonathan, while Katie teased him about the alfalfa sprout incident.

"Alfalfa sprout incident?" Jonathan slapped his knee. "You make it sound like a Robert Ludlum suspense novel!"

"Well, it *was* pretty exciting," Eric pointed out.

"Speaking of suspense, this is a great movie,"

Diana turned to Katie. "Right at the beginning — "

Jeremy clapped a hand tenderly over his pretty girl friend's mouth. "She's seen it already, and she's determined to ruin it for the rest of us," he explained in his soft British accent.

Diana shook her long blonde hair; all innocence. "I just wanted to give you some background, that's all!"

Fiona laughed. "You are really safer sitting at least five rows away."

"Don't listen to her," Diana said, with a good-natured smile.

"So what are you two up to this weekend?" Jonathan asked Eric.

Eric shrugged. "Don't really know yet."

When Jeremy mentioned that the four of them were planning to go to the crew team's race the next day and invited them to join the outing, Katie looked at Eric eagerly. It would be a good chance to see for herself if she liked crew. It was supposed to be a beautiful day — perfect for hanging out by the river.

She thought she might have to talk him into it because of his attitude on the way over tonight, but he agreed right away. They decided they'd all meet on the river bank at ten.

Back in their own row, Katie and Eric snuggled together deep in their seats and propped their knees up against the seats in front of them. Eric leaned over and kissed Katie's ear.

"I'm sorry I was kind of a jerk back there in the car," he said. "You know I love everything you do. You're a champ and I'm proud of you.

We'll check out this crew business together, okay?"

"Okay." Katie was satisfied. Eric really did want her to do her own thing. And he hadn't been unreasonable to worry a *little* about the amount of time they got to spend together. They'd never really had enough, but it didn't need to be an issue between them. They'd learned to make the most of what they did have.

When the movie started, Katie put her head on Eric's shoulder. His arm was snug around her and his fingers stroking her hair were soothing. She sighed. She was comfortable. Eric was comfortable. She'd gotten so used to being near him like this that she almost felt more like herself this way than she did when she was alone.

She reached for the popcorn and her hand bumped into Eric's. Their fingers interlocked and they ended up holding hands for the rest of the movie. As the minutes passed, Katie was almost able to forget the irritation she'd felt on the drive over when Eric had gotten bossy about crew. But there was a little something, a very tiny something nagging at the back of her mind. Katie let the movie absorb her attention.

When the film ended and the lights came up, Jeremy, Diana, Fiona, and Jonathan joined them. "Sub shop?" Jonathan suggested, slinging his arm around Fiona's slender shoulders. "I'm craving a cheeseburger special like you wouldn't believe!" Fiona grimaced.

"Onion rings!" added Jeremy enthusiastically.

Eric started to say yes even as Katie blurted

out an emphatic no. When the others, including Eric, looked at her in surprise, she smiled sheepishly and shrugged.

"Um, Eric, I thought we could just go for a drive or something. I'm not really hungry."

Eric tugged on her ponytail and winked at the others. "Whatever you say, K.C. Sounds pretty good to me."

Katie was actually starving and the mention of onion rings made her mouth water, but suddenly the last place she wanted to be was the sub shop. It was everyone's favorite hangout and there was sure to be a huge crowd from Kennedy there. Maybe even Greg Montgomery. She had to admit to herself that was why she didn't want to go. She had a feeling that if she saw Greg tonight, when she was with Eric, the little niggling thing in the back of her mind that she couldn't put her finger on might get bigger. It would be better for her and Eric to spend some time alone. There wouldn't be anything — or anybody — to get in the way of her feelings that way.

Without saying anything to Katie, Eric headed the car north. Soon they were pulling between the old stone pillars that marked the entrance to Rosemont Park. Eric drove past the formal gardens and parked at the overlook.

They sat for a few moments in silence gazing out at the sparkling night vista. The Potomac River was shining in the moonlight below them and the Washington Monument glowed softly in the distance. Katie sighed deeply. Eric reached for her and she jumped a little. She hadn't sighed because being alone with Eric at the overlook stirred romantic feelings in her. Right now she wanted more assurance of their togetherness than she could get from a kiss. She needed to talk.

She put a hand on Eric's shoulder and pushed him away gently but firmly. He looked surprised and she hurried to offer an explanation. "Um, maybe we should go. I told my parents I'd be home by, uh, ten."

Eric raised an eyebrow. "Ten? On a Friday night?"

Katie shrugged and then giggled. "No, maybe not. I just thought, well, we could go now."

As Eric brushed the hair gently back from her forehead, his own forehead creased with concern. "But we just got here." He smiled suggestively. "You were the one who wanted to go for a 'drive.' "

She smiled and then sighed again. "I know. I guess I'm just . . . tired."

Eric kissed her lightly. "Then why don't I take you home."

"Okay."

As they drove back through the park Katie found herself feeling more and more stifled by the companionable silence between them. She wanted Eric to say something — anything — that would reaffirm their closeness, the fact that they knew each other better than anybody else could.

Eric, meanwhile, seemed completely unperturbed. He whistled cheerfully as he steered the car through the gates and onto Oakland Avenue.

Well, Katie thought to herself, I guess it's not fair to expect him to read my mind. We're not Siamese twins. Just boyfriend and girl friend. She cleared her throat.

"So, have you worked any more on your college applications?" she asked. She and Eric and most of their junior and senior friends had gone to the College Night held at Kennedy earlier that week. There were presentations by dozens of schools and Katie and Eric had both picked up handfuls of brochures.

"I'm still working on an essay. I want it to be one that sort of jumps out and grabs you, you know?" He grinned. "It's gotta say, 'Take me!' "

Katie laughed. "So far my essay just says, 'I'm a good kid just like everybody else.' "

Eric put a hand on her knee and gave it a pat. "But you're not just like everyone else," he said sincerely. "You're special. That'll come through."

"Thanks."

"Wasn't that Williams College presentation great, though?" Eric's voice became enthusiastic. "I'm really psyched to go up there for an interview next month."

Katie nodded. "It sounds like a nice school. But isn't it kind of small?"

"Yeah, but that's what I like about it."

Katie tucked her knees up and put her feet on the dashboard. "That's not for me. I want someplace *big!* Someplace where there's something happening every day, where I'll never stop meeting new people."

Eric laughed and Katie realized they were

starting one of their typical college discussions — small liberal arts versus big university, country versus city, the usual. They had the opposite opinion on every point. Usually she had fun debating her side against Eric's. Tonight, though, she got a cold feeling in her stomach and a lump in her throat. Suddenly their difference of opinion about college wasn't just amusing. She saw it for what it really meant, that in the natural course of things, she and Eric really might not always be together.

She wished she'd kept her mouth shut. Talking had only made her more unsettled. She wasn't quite sure why, but she felt kind of scared and sad. She looked at Eric, sitting a foot away from her, and he seemed very far away.

They pulled up to her house. Katie could see that the light in her parents' bedroom was still on. Phew, they're still up, she thought. She and Eric couldn't sit for an hour in the car then.

She turned and put her arms around him. He hugged her close. "Sorry I pooped out so early," she said, her voice muffled against his red plaid flannel shirt.

"That's okay," he said. She felt him kiss the top of her head lightly. For some reason that caused a tear to spring to her eye.

Before he could see it, she hopped from the car. "I'll see you in the morning!" she said brightly. "Love you!"

"I love you, too," Eric called after her.

"G'night!"

"G'night!"

Katie closed the front door quietly behind her. She hoped Eric didn't mind that she'd skipped out on a good-night kiss. She'd been afraid to share one with him. Tonight, kissing Eric good-night would have felt more like kissing him good-bye.

Chapter

3

Diana closed her eyes and took a deep breath. She tipped her face toward the sun and shook her long hair. "I love fall!" she exclaimed.

It was a glorious day. The sky was so blue, the trees were so vivid, and the lawn stretching down to the river was so green, it almost looked to Katie like a touched-up photograph. Too beautiful to be true.

She sat cross-legged on the big blanket Molly had brought with her, leaning with one elbow on somebody's picnic basket. Eric was there, too, as well as Jeremy, Fiona, and Jonathan. Katie had called Elise Hammond that morning, and she'd said she would try to come, too, if she could talk her boyfriend, Ben Forrest, into coming with her.

Katie felt as sunny as the day. She'd woken up laughing at herself for being so neurotic the night before. Her life was fine. It was a blast being with her friends. She couldn't be happier!

Molly pushed back the bright orange scarf knotted in her curly hair and turned to Katie. "This was such a fantastic idea!" she said. "Who gets the credit?"

"I'm not sure," answered Katie. "Probably Mr. Social Director." She leaned forward and gave Jonathan a playful slap on the shoulder. Jonathan was Kennedy's student activities director. He could dream up a creative fundraising scheme or a wacky prom theme just as fast as he could drum up support from his classmates — and he really had a knack for recruiting volunteers.

"Well, whoever's idea it was, it was a great one. I almost don't need this heavy sweater!" Molly pushed up the sleeves of her bulky pullover. Underneath it her arms were still tan. She lay back on the blanket. "Sunbathing time!" she declared, sighing with contentment.

Eric held his hands up to block the rays from Molly's face. "Time out," he called. "Summer's over!"

"No, it's not," Molly insisted. She sat up and swatted his hands away. "Look at Susan and Rich. They've got the right idea."

Katie and Eric both looked at where Molly was pointing. Susan Atkinson and Rich Edwards, both in bright white tennis outfits, were standing on the dock talking to Greg. Katie knew Rich was pretty good friends with Greg. Rich gave his buddy a good-luck slap on the shoulder and then grabbed Susan's hand — the one that wasn't holding a tennis racket — and headed up the bank toward the group on the blanket.

Her friends greeted the newcomers, but Katie's eyes stayed glued on Greg. He was surrounded by seven tall boys, a few of whom she recognized from school. His face was serious — intense — and he gestured with his hands as he spoke. Pep talk, Katie thought, amused.

He was still facing in her direction, and now he looked up. From where she sat, Katie could see his eyes light up with pleasure as his gaze met hers. He flashed her a bright smile that made her feel warm all over. Katie realized she'd been looking forward to seeing him again. And there was really nothing wrong with that — he was an acquaintance who she hoped was on his way to becoming a friend.

The red and gold uniformed Kennedy team put their boat in the water, and the Leesburg and Hinsdale teams followed them after Greg's crew had paddled away from the dock. Katie studied the rowers. One boy was a lot smaller than the others. That must be the coxswain, she thought with interest.

She watched as they warmed up by rowing upstream to the starting line. Then she leaned against Eric and snuggled her head against his shoulder.

"Are you sure you can see that way?" Eric asked. He gave her a hug. "Why don't you sit up?"

"But I'm so comfortable!" Katie protested. "And I can see well enough. How much is there to see, anyway? They're way out in the river, and they'll eventually row by, right?"

"Haven't you ever been to a crew race?" Jonathan asked.

"No," Katie admitted.

"And this is the girl who thinks she wants to be a cox!" Eric teased.

Molly looked at her friend in surprise. "You do? Since when?"

"Since yesterday," Katie said. "Greg Montgomery's trying to talk me into it."

"Hmmm," Molly commented, her big blue eyes dancing. "He could talk *me* into anything he wanted to, that's for sure!"

"Oh, you!" Katie shook her head and smiled. Even though she was true-blue faithful to her boyfriend, Ted Mason, who was a freshman in college, Molly had always been and always would be an incorrigible flirt.

"Well, I'd definitely suggest that you sit up, then," said Jonathan, pushing up the brim of his gray Indiana Jones-style fedora. "This might be more exciting than you think."

A few minutes later, Katie, Molly, Eric, Jonathan, and the rest of the gang were on their feet, shouting at the tops of their lungs. The race was so close — the three boats were almost perfectly matched. They ran abreast until a few yards from the finish line when the Hinsdale boat pulled ahead. Leesburg beat Kennedy by half a boat length.

Katie was breathless from cheering. The boats had looked so beautiful, cutting across the surface of the water like knives. She wanted to do that! And they were fast—they really flew. As the boats for the second race rowed up the river to the starting line, she watched the coxswain carefully. During the first race, the Kennedy cox

31

had leaned forward slightly in a stiff pose and was loudly calling out commands. It was lot more complicated than just "Stroke! Stroke!" Katie couldn't wait to ask Greg some of the questions that were popping into her mind.

"What do you think?"

Katie turned in surprise to see Eric watching her. For a moment she'd forgotten she wasn't alone with her thoughts.

She smiled sheepishly, knowing her enthusiasm was written all over her face. "It's neat," she said, taking his hand and pulling him down on the blanket beside her. "Didn't you think so?"

"Yeah," Eric admitted. He picked up a yellow-veined maple leaf from the grass and tucked it carefully behind her right ear. "That was a pretty intense race." He was silent for a moment. "You're not still thinking of joining the team, are you?"

Katie turned her head sharply. "Of course I am!" she exclaimed. "Even more now than I was before." She frowned, puzzled. "Why shouldn't I?"

"I didn't mean that you shouldn't," he amended. He appeared to be concentrating overly hard on retying the shoelace of one of his torn basketball sneakers.

"Well, what *did* you mean?" Katie demanded, more curious than annoyed.

"I'm not sure," Eric shrugged. "I'm just not sure it's a good idea."

"And why is that?"

"Look, forget it." He waved a hand in exasperation. "I just think what I think."

"Well, what you're thinking doesn't make much sense to me," she said, miffed. "If you're thinking I shouldn't join crew just because Greg Montgomery had something to do with it — "

Before Katie could finish her thoughts or Eric could respond, they were distracted. Jonathan waved his arms to get everybody's attention and then tossed his hat in the air.

Fiona raised a hand to her mouth. "Don't look now," she whispered in her British accent, "but I think he's been struck by another inspiration."

"I've got it!" Jonathan declared, his gray eyes gleaming. Everyone groaned and rolled their eyes. Jonathan looked at them, pretending to be offended. "Now, is that any way to react when your fearless leader comes up with an idea for a great new project?"

"Well, let's hear it!" Jeremy urged. Susan grabbed Rich and he let her wrestle him down onto the blanket. Molly giggled.

"Well, I'll tell you, even though you don't deserve to hear it. How about. . . ." Jonathan paused deliberately. The group groaned again and he grinned. "How about building an all-school event," he continued, "around one of the crew team's races? It would be a good way to gain more support for the sport and as the skimpy turnout today demonstrates" — he gestured at the few people scattered on the river bank — "it could use it. And we could have a lot of fun at the same time!"

"Fun, maybe," conceded Rich. "I mean, watching these races today *is* fun. But where do you get *a lot* of fun?"

Jonathan waved a hand again. "Look around. What do you see? Lots of grass. Fantastic fall weather. Plenty of room for a full-scale October Festival — concession booths, a band, anything we want!"

Jonathan's proposal was met by eager nods. In a minute everyone was tossing around ideas. Katie joined the clamor, mischievously suggesting that if they held this free-for-all on Halloween weekend, maybe the members of the crew teams could row in costumes.

"What do you think Montgomery's going to think about all this?" Rich wondered aloud.

"About what?" Greg asked, joining the group. After everyone told him what a close race they had just rowed, Greg slung an arm across Susan's shoulders and she pushed him away, wrinkling her nose in mock disgust.

"You may be a crew hero, but you're an awfully sweaty one."

Greg laughed. "Fill me in, Edwards!"

While Rich recounted the discussion, Katie tried her best not to stare openly at Greg. If it was possible, he looked even better than he had yesterday in the weight room. His rowing tank left his well-muscled shoulders bare. His tanned skin was gleaming and his eyes, narrowed against the bright sun, were the color of the water at Ocean City.

"So what you've got in mind is some kind of Kennedy High Invitational Regatta at the end of the season," Greg said to Jonathan. He glanced at Katie, one corner of his mouth lifting in a friendly smile. She looked away hurriedly.

"Exactly!" Jonathan dropped a hand on Greg's broad shoulder. "That's the ticket. If you can line up some teams to participate, the committee — that's everyone here right now, folks — will take care of the rest!"

Greg nodded thoughtfully. "I think we've got a deal!"

The committee agreed to meet again soon to delegate responsibilities. To Katie's relief, Greg jogged back down to the dock to get his team ready for the next race. She'd been having a hard time trying not to look at him, afraid of what another one of his smiles would do to her. At the same time, she was avoiding Eric's gaze in case he should notice her confusion.

"Hey, K.C." Molly shook her arm gently. "Calling all cars! Are you there?"

Katie blinked and then laughed. "Thanks for waking me up. I guess I was daydreaming."

"I'll say. Want to walk down to the bridge and watch the last race from there?"

"Sure!" Katie answered, eager to escape the group scene. As she turned to go, she spoke to Eric. "Be right back."

"Okay," he said, without much animation.

The two girls walked along the river bank in silence for a few moments. Katie dug her hands deep in the pockets of her jeans, wondering how and if she should tell Molly what was on her mind.

Molly beat her to it. She bent down and grabbed a handful of leaves and tossed them at her friend. "Spill the beans, K.C.! What's up?"

Katie brushed the leaves off her sweater and giggled. "Was I that obvious?"

"Just to me," Molly assured her.

Katie sighed. "Well, Moll, it's like this. . . ." She hesitated. "Do you think it's possible to *sort* of fall in love at first sight" — Molly smiled, and Katie could tell she was thinking about Ted — "and kind of fall *out* of love with another person just as fast?"

Molly's smile faded. "Whoa. Did something happen between you and Eric?"

Katie shook her head. "Not really." The two stepped onto the bridge and walked a few yards, then leaned their elbows on the railing and gazed downstream. Katie told Molly about her afternoon with Greg and her evening with Eric, and Eric's unfair and jealous responses to her plan to try crew.

Molly whistled and then laughed at Katie's serious face. "Relax! You really don't have anything to worry about."

Katie looked hopeful. "I don't?"

"Definitely not," Molly said emphatically. "It's too soon to panic about changing feelings for Eric or a crush on Greg," she continued. "And anyway, it's pretty natural to sometimes be less than excited about your boyfriend and to find somebody else attractive, you know." Her voice was so matter-of-fact and reassuring that Katie instantly felt better. "In another twenty-four hours," Molly added, "you might make a complete turnaround. Give yourself a chance."

Katie pulled a leaf from her sweater and

dropped it into the river. She watched it twirl downward, then get swept aside by a current of air, before settling onto the surface of the water.

"You're right, Molly." She turned and gave her friend a hug. "Thanks."

"Just take a deep breath and count to ten," Molly advised. "It works for me every time."

"Greg sure is cute," Katie reminded her.

Molly winked. "Okay, count to twenty!"

When the races were over, Molly and Katie headed back down to the river bank where the gang was delving into the huge picnic basket Diana and Fiona had packed. Molly grabbed an apple and sat down on the edge of the blanket.

She tried to tune in to the chatter around her — Jonathan was teasing Fiona about her leather pants; Katie and Eric were talking quietly; Ben and Elise were making plans for the evening — but she found herself feeling suddenly different and apart from the rest of the gang. Why bother trying to tune in? she thought ruefully. I'm not on the same frequency.

Hearing Katie talk about Eric and Greg had reminded Molly that she was practically the only one of her girl friends right now who didn't have a boyfriend. Holly, too, was without her boyfriend Bart. But Holly was so caught up in her studies and her plans for going to college premed that she didn't have *time* to miss Bart.

Of course Molly had Ted, but he was at college, too, and at a moment like this, he might as well have been on the moon. In fact, now that she thought about it, their situation was a lot like Greg Montgomery's and Chris Austin's. Chris had graduated and Greg was left behind. But from everything Molly had seen and from what Katie had told her, it certainly seemed like those two were going their separate ways, as if it was inevitable that they would.

Molly took a big bite out of her apple and crunched it, wondering what it was all going to mean for her and Ted. When he'd left for college she hadn't questioned their commitment. They cared for each other — that was all that mattered. Their love would take care of itself. After all, their relationship had already made it through a lot. They'd been separated before. After the summer they met on the beach in Ocean City, she'd had to go back to California. And when she and her mom first moved to Rose Hill, things were rocky for a while.

She bit into her apple again and grimaced. All of a sudden it tasted sour. She tossed it into a nearby trashcan. I'm the one that's sour, she acknowledged silently. I'm just a crabapple. Lighten up, Ramirez!

She jumped into the debate Diana and Jeremy were having about whether Bruce Springsteen and the E Street Band were really greater than the Beatles, but her mind was still on Ted. She missed him a lot, and up until now she'd always felt they had a strong relationship. Before she and Ted had started seeing each other she used to date a lot, and she'd dated last year when she was in California and Ted was in Rose Hill. This time around she didn't have any desire to date anybody else, even casually.

The others had stood up and were stretching, getting ready to go. Molly folded her blanket and tucked it under her arm. She thought about Ted at college and herself at Kennedy High. Was she making a mistake thinking they could still belong to each other?

Chapter
4

Greg looked at the clock over the door of his history classroom for at least the tenth time that period. He tapped the pencil impatiently on his notebook. This was definitely the longest and most boring lecture Mr. Novato had ever given. The Civil War itself was probably over in less time!

He looked at the clock again and then at his watch. He couldn't remember a Monday ever going by so slowly. He really wasn't sure he was going to make it until the final bell, even though it was only ten minutes away.

He couldn't remember ever being so eager for school to end — and crew practice to start. He'd called Katie Crawford at home last night to invite her along, and she had agreed to join him and the rest of the guys in the school parking lot, where they met three afternoons a week to carpool to the river for practice. Greg couldn't wait to see her again.

He pushed the sandy hair back from his forehead with his left hand and doodled a cartoon of Mr. Novato in the margin of his notebook with his right. Ever since Friday, when he'd bumped into her at the school gym, he hadn't been able to get Katie out of his mind. He wasn't quite sure why. Sure, she was cute. Definitely very cute. And fun, nice . . . like a lot of girls at school. That's kind of what he'd always thought about her — not that he'd ever thought much about her before this — that she was just one of the girls. But now she'd come to his attention with more force than Kirsten Berg had, who'd been pretty exotic. He couldn't quite figure it out.

The bell rang. Greg jumped out of his seat and made it to the door before Mr. Novato had time to turn around from the blackboard to dismiss the class. He sprinted down the hall, skidded around the corner, clattered his locker open, banged it closed again, ran to the gym and changed his clothes, and was outside and across the parking lot leaning against his mom's white Mercedes in under ten minutes. He was panting slightly as he unlocked the door and tossed his backpack inside. He'd begged his mother to let him have the car that morning — he wanted to be the one to drive Katie to practice.

He slammed the door shut and straightened up, then bent over to pull down one of the legs of his sweat pants, which had ridden up to his knee. He resisted the urge to check his hair in the car mirror. That was really going too far.

When he saw Katie approaching with Aaron Silver, one of his best rowers, Greg couldn't suppress the surge of pleasure that ran through him. There was no point denying to himself that Katie was the reason he was so pumped up for practice today. This wasn't just any girl.

His eyes met hers. He could see them sparkle across the parking lot. Her glance reminded him of how much she'd impressed him when she stood up during the funding hearing last spring to ardently defend the gymnastics team. Her big brown eyes had flashed, and he was able to tell she felt the same way about her sport as he did about crew. She had drive and ambition — like he did himself.

And like his girl friend, Chris, had. In fact, the other day in the weight room, talking to Katie in depth for the first time, Greg had been struck by how much she resembled Chris in that respect. But only in that way. Chris was cool and sophisticated — she was two years older than he was, and she'd often made him feel like he had to act older. Katie, on the other hand, was warm and spontaneous and somehow . . . *young*. And now, when she greeted him with a bright hello and a sweet smile, Greg's ordinarily imperturbable stomach flip-flopped like a lovestruck thirteen-year-old's.

"Hey, Katie," he responded lightly. He took her bookbag from her and opened the passenger door. "You need a ride, don't you?"

"Yeah, do you mind?"

"Of course not! Hop in."

Aaron had continued on down the lot. "I've got a car today, Greg," he called back over his shoulder. "I'll wait for Carl and Timmy, and we'll see you over there."

"Sounds good."

Greg got in the car and turned to look at Katie. She put on her seat belt and looked back at him. They sat that way for a minute until Greg remembered that he was supposed to be starting the car and driving someplace.

He backed out of the parking space quickly, but inside him a little voice was saying, Whoa. This is another guy's girl friend. Cool it! He might be free now himself, but he knew that Katie wasn't. When Chris had come home a few weeks ago, they'd gone out to dinner and talked for hours. It had been hard to make their separation official because he still cared about her, but it was what they both wanted, under the circumstances. It was difficult to ignore, however, that Katie was still half of a well-known Kennedy couple.

Greg followed Main Street to River Road, answering all of Katie's questions about crew. When they pulled up at the boathouse he climbed out of the car, steeling himself to look at her objectively. She was just a new member of his team. It was no good letting his imagination run away with him.

As he led Katie to the boathouse, though, he realized it was going to be hard not to. She was so bright and enthusiastic, listening intently as

43

he explained the different parts of the shell to her and the responsibilities of each rower, particularly the coxswain's.

After what he jokingly called the anatomy lesson, Greg and two of the other boys carried the shell over their heads from the boathouse to the water's edge. "In a lot of ways, the coxswain is the most important member of the team," he said to Katie, who was walking at his side.

"How can the smallest person be the most important?" she wondered. "The cox doesn't even have oars!"

"Easy." Greg grunted as they rolled the boat down to their waists and carefully lowered it into the water. "The cox is like a coach. Although you don't row, you have to know *how* to. You have to correct what your rowers are doing wrong, as well as steer the boat. Then there's race strategy, and knowing when to go for it. You saw our race the other day, didn't you?" Katie nodded, her red ponytail bouncing. "Well, it was close and we gave it everything we had, but we lost it. In a case like that, a good cox can make the difference."

Katie looked around her. "Where is your cox anyway?"

"He's going to work with the second boat today. I'm taking a gamble on you and putting you in my strongest boat." He grinned. "With me. Where I can keep an eye on you."

Katie wrinkled her nose. "Well, if I steer you right into the cattails on the other side of the river, don't say I didn't warn you!"

Greg laughed. "You'll do fine. Anyway, I

don't expect you to learn everything in one day, and you shouldn't expect it of yourself. Just concentrate on picking up a few of the basics — getting comfortable in the boat and getting a feel for the rowing rhythm." He looked at her speculatively. "How's your voice, anyway?"

Katie giggled. "You heard it the other day, remember?"

Greg hooted. "That's right! You're a Bruce Springsteen sound-alike. Don't worry. You'll make a great coxswain!"

"Gee, thanks. I'll take that as a compliment."

Greg held her eye for a long moment. "Please do."

Katie blushed and turned back to the shell. "So what do I do?"

Greg turned to look over his shoulder. "Over here!" He waved a hand to Aaron and Carl, who were carrying a small shell over their heads. "Katie, we're going to try it in this little boat first. Just you, me, and Aaron in a coxed pair — okay?"

"Okay!"

He slipped into the boat from the dock and held out a hand to her. "All aboard!"

Katie smiled and saluted him. "Aye, aye, Captain!"

She climbed in the boat, her legs a little bit shaky. As soon as she was sitting comfortably in position, her knees almost up to her chin, Greg and Aaron stroked the boat onto the river and started the lesson. Greg did a pretty good job of explaining the workings of the rudder that rested behind the coxswain's back and was operated by two strings with wooden "knockers" on the ends, one for each of the coxswain's hands. But at moments it was all he could do to remember which end was the bow and which was the stern. Katie looked so adorable perched in front of him in the coxswain's seat, carefully taking in all of his instructions.

And she learned fast. He was ridiculously proud of her. Later in the afternoon they took a run with three other rowers in a four, something Greg hadn't expected she'd be ready to do until the next practice.

"You were terrific," Aaron congratulated Katie at the end of the afternoon.

"She's really gonna go places, huh?" Greg agreed enthusiastically.

"So long as she takes us with her," Aaron joked.

"Aw, pshaw," Katie said. "You guys are the ones that really make it work." She started pulling her sweat pants on over her shorts. The late afternoon air was getting just a little chilly.

"Um, Katie, before you do that," Aaron began, glancing at a few of the other guys standing near them on the dock. He gestured casually in Katie's direction and they smiled broadly. "There's a tradition that comes with being a new member of the crew team. I really think you oughta experience it."

"What's that?" Katie asked, her eyes wide and innocent.

She figured it out as soon as John Cannon and Aaron grabbed her. She barely had time to squeal,

"Greg, save me!" before they tossed her into the water.

She came to the surface laughing, and Greg grabbed her hands to haul her back up on the dock. He couldn't help grinning. "Sorry, K.C.," he said apologetically. "Just a little ritual."

Katie shook her head and water flew from her dripping ponytail. She grinned right back at him. "As long as you can promise me it doesn't happen every day!"

Greg put an arm around her. "Promise. Come on, there's a blanket in the back of my car. Practice is over. See you guys on Wednesday."

As they walked to the car together Greg smiled to himself, thinking how differently Chris would have reacted if *she'd* been dumped in the river. No doubt about it, she would have been furious. She wouldn't have forgiven him for a week.

And there was no doubt about something else, he thought as he bundled Katie up in the blanket and settled her in the front seat. She was even cuter soaking wet. He had to restrain an urge to wrap not only the blanket, but his arms around her as well.

"Now it's your turn to tell me where you live," Greg said.

"Magnolia Street. Take a left here." Katie instructed.

It was an overcast afternoon, and it was already getting dark when Greg pulled over in front of Katie's house. He hoped she wouldn't jump right out of the car and run inside and she didn't. They

47

sat and talked and laughed for half an hour. She told him a story about her first gymnastics meet for Kennedy, when she did a split on the balance beam and split her leotard at the same time, and he told one about winning a tennis match at his club and catching his toe and falling flat on his face when he tried to jump over the net to shake his opponent's hand. She asked him about his summer job at Congressman Barnes' office, and he confided that he hoped someday to go into politics himself. She confessed to a secret dream of being a restaurant critic for the *Washington Post*. "Or an Olympic coxswain," she joked.

Greg watched Katie's face as she talked. It was so animated, it made him feel warm and happy just to look at her. He hadn't felt like this since . . . since he first met Chris, he realized. Even Kirsten hadn't touched him quite this way.

He knew he should say good-bye to Katie and drive home. It wasn't right to sit here and have feelings like this for another guy's girl friend. Although, maybe that's hypocritical of me, he thought wryly. After all, he and Chris had fallen in love when she was still seeing Ted Mason.

As he looked into Katie's warm, dark eyes, all Greg's good intentions melted away. And he was sure he wasn't imagining the look in those eyes, either — she was experiencing all the same sensations he was.

They stopped talking and just sat looking at each other. Greg couldn't resist leaning closer to Katie. He put an arm around her and her gaze didn't falter. The emotion in her eyes even seemed to deepen. He put one hand gently on the back of her neck and brought his face close to hers. When he began to kiss her she responded warmly. The longer he held her, the more passion he felt flow between them.

When the kiss ended Katie lowered her eyes and buried her face in Greg's chest. He still had his arms around her and now he reached for the door and pushed down the lock.

"There, now you're my prisoner," he said. "I won't let you go until you kiss me like that again."

"Oh, Greg," Katie whispered. Her voice was small and suddenly she seemed very tiny in his arms.

"What's the matter?" he asked quietly. "Wasn't that nice?"

She shook her head. "It was very nice."

"But it was the wrong thing to do."

"No." Katie raised her eyes and smiled weakly. "It just makes things . . . hard."

He touched her cheek with his finger. The tremor in her voice made him feel guilty. "I'm sorry, K.C. I don't want to make you unhappy."

She shook her head again. Her eyes were still glowing. "You don't. Believe me." She wriggled out of the blanket and tossed it into the back-seat. She shivered. "I'd better go. It was kind of a cold day for a swim, now that I think of it."

Greg put a hand on either side of her flushed face. "You'll be okay?"

"Sure," she said. She unlocked the door and swung it open. "I'll see you Wednesday, right?"

"Yeah. Wednesday. 'Bye, Katie."

She smiled. " 'Bye, Greg."

He watched her jog up the driveway, and then turn to wave as she opened the front door. He honked the horn and headed for his house. When he flipped the radio on, Bruce Springsteen was singing Katie's favorite song. Greg grinned and started singing along. He wasn't sure what he and Katie might be getting into, but it sure felt good.

Chapter
5

Still in a daze, Katie wiped her feet mechanically on the Welcome mat and stepped into her house. Even at the most tense moment of gymnastics' competition her knees had never felt this weak. She didn't know how she'd made it up the driveway without tripping, knowing Greg was watching her.

There was only one thing she was sure about right now. No one had made her feel the way she'd felt this afternoon in Greg's car. Not that she'd kissed very many boys. In fact, Katie acknowledged to herself as she flopped down on her bed with her math book, she'd only kissed Eric. But even Eric hadn't had quite such an effect on her.

A couple of hours later she could still feel the heat of Greg's arms around her. All evening she'd been half floating on air and half dragging her feet. She was dreading her nightly phone call with Eric. It was only a matter of time. She knew if she didn't call him, he'd call her. Even more, she dreaded seeing him the next day in school. How could she face him?

The phone rang and Katie jumped. Her math book flew out of her hands, and she knew even before she heard her brother, Danny, shouting for her that it was Eric.

She walked slowly down the hall to her parents' bedroom and stared at the telephone on the night table for a long moment before picking it up.

"I've got it!" she yelled to her brother. When she heard the click, she said, "Hello?"

"Hi, Katie. It's me."

"Hi, Eric!"

It was easier than she expected to chatter cheerfully for five minutes with Eric. They hadn't seen each other all day, and he told her he'd missed her. Katie felt a pang of guilt when he said that. She hadn't had time to miss him. He'd been the farthest thing from her mind until she'd gotten home that evening.

After Katie gave him a brief — very brief — account of the afternoon's crew practice, Eric started talking at length about the preseason meeting of the boys' swim team. Katie had a chance to collect her thoughts. She swallowed hard. She knew she couldn't hang up the phone leaving Eric thinking there was nothing wrong. She sat on her parents' bed, thinking rapidly. She didn't notice when Eric stopped talking on the other end until he broke the silence by saying, "Katie?"

She gripped the phone tightly. "I'm still here, Eric."

"Where'd you go to?" His voice was teasing, and Katie could almost see him smiling. "Thought I'd lost you for a minute there."

Katie sighed. "Sorry."

Eric waited, and when she didn't say anything further, he asked, "Is something bothering you?"

"Yeah, something is." Katie pulled the black and orange Orioles jersey she wore as a nightgown down over her knees. She resisted an urge to say good-bye and hang up the phone. She had no idea what she was going to say next.

"A problem with Coach Romanski or your training?" he guessed. "Or are you stumped on your applications? I'm having some trouble with mine. Wanna talk about it?" He sounded caring but not overly concerned, and Katie saw an easy way out.

"I do want to talk," she admitted. "But . . . it's nothing much. It can wait."

"You sure you don't want me to come over?" he offered.

"Uh, no," Katie said hastily. "It's late. I'll see you tomorrow at lunch, okay?"

"All right," Eric's voice was light. He clearly wasn't worried about their relationship. Katie squeezed her eyes shut. She had to get off the phone before she burst out crying or laughing or something else.

"And Katie," Eric added, "I love you."

"I love you, too," Katie said softly. She felt hollow inside as soon as she'd said it. "Goodnight."

" 'Night, K.C."

Katie trotted back to her room, wrapped herself up in her bedspread, and shivered. She propped herself up in bed, then tilted her head back and stared at the ceiling. By telling Eric she wanted to talk, she had taken a step she couldn't take back. She'd committed herself to something, but what?

She leaned over and reached a hand under her bed to pull out the cloth-covered notebook she used as a journal. She opened to the page marked by a pen — the last entry she'd made. A whole week ago! Before she'd met Greg at the weight room, before she went to crew practice. . . . So much had happened since then.

She read the last words she'd written — a description of an especially satisfying gymnastics session with her coach, a date for dinner with Eric. . . . She stared at the words on the page. She wished she could climb right inside her journal and experience the feelings she'd recorded there. That dinner with Eric seemed like a million years ago. The girl who'd written those words couldn't be her.

She picked up the pen and touched it lightly to the paper. She wanted to write about what was happening to her now. Maybe if she put her thoughts down it would help straighten out things in her mind. She still cared for Eric — he was special to her, he'd always be special to her. They'd shared so much, and he was the first boy she had ever loved. She knew, too, that his feelings for her hadn't changed. But she also knew she couldn't ignore what had taken place between her and Greg that afternoon.

Katie focused on the page and when she saw that she'd sketched a big question mark, she slammed the little book shut with a groan of frustration. Looking up, she met the eyes of her favorite sports heroines staring down at her from posters on the wall over her desk. Too bad I don't have a famous problem-solver up there, she thought grimly.

It was only nine-thirty, but Katie crawled into bed, anyway. She felt better buried deep under the blankets with her stuffed Paddington, sheltered from everything and everyone outside her room. She thought about seeing Eric at lunch the next day and immediately considered staying in her bed indefinitely. She could say she was sick. She might as well be — she certainly *felt* sick when she imagined an encounter with Eric.

But she couldn't hide forever.

Katie reached over to flip off the light switch. She lay awake a long time in the darkened room, studying the weird shadows cast by the moonlight and wondering what she was going to say to Eric. Not much came to mind. She could only hope that the words would just come to her, and that when they did they'd be the *right* words.

Katie didn't often wish her classes would last forever, but the next morning she sat in French the period before lunch doing exactly that. She watched the clock and mentally willed it to stop — but to no avail. When the bell rang, she gathered her books together at a snail's pace and then spent a full minute fiddling with the buckle of her bookbag.

Molly was standing in the doorway, tapping one sneakered foot. "What are you doing, K.C.?" she asked, impatiently, pushing the left strap of her baby blue overalls back up on her shoulder. "Breathing in the last breath of knowledge from the air here? I suppose there might be a few more irregular verbs floating around."

"Excuse me!" Katie said. She forced a smile for her friend. "Let's just say I'm not in a hurry to get to lunch today."

"No kidding!" Molly exclaimed. She saw the look on Katie's face and her tone changed. "I'm just teasing you, Katie. Is something the matter?"

Katie joined her at the door, and they started down the bustling hall toward the cafeteria. "Yeah, something is. And I've never had something like this the matter with me!"

Molly frowned, her blue eyes narrowing with concern. "Is it Eric again?"

"Yep." Katie glanced around her before speaking in a low voice. "I don't have time to tell you everything now, Moll. I'll talk to you after school. But basically something happened yesterday with Greg — I was going to call you — and Eric and I are going to have to talk — "

Her voice broke and she stopped in her tracks. Molly gripped both of Katie's arms with her hands. "Katie, are you sure you're ready for this? You don't *sound* as if you are."

Katie sniffled. "I'm as ready as I'll ever be, I

guess. I mean, I don't know what I'm getting ready *for!*" She laughed and shook her head dismissively. "Don't worry, Moll. I'm probably making a mountain out of a molehill. After all, what could really happen?"

Molly pushed open the cafeteria door. "Yeah, what could really happen?"

Katie wasn't sure, but when she sat down at the gang's usual table in the north corner and saw the solemn expression on Eric's face she realized she'd been wrong to imagine for a minute that she and Eric were going to get together to talk amiably about the weather.

He didn't greet her with the usual hug and kiss, although he'd saved her a chair next to him. She pulled her ham and swiss sandwich out of her lunch bag. Eric poked without much interest at the macaroni and cheese on his tray. His forehead was creased. Katie didn't often see him looking so preoccupied.

They both ate quickly and neither said much. Katie didn't even pretend to care about the conversation her other friends were having, although they were talking about the October Festival Regatta. She didn't comment when Jonathan appointed her Greg's assistant for the crew part and also the paper plate and plastic cup chairman.

"Wanna take a walk, Katie?" Eric finally asked quietly.

Katie nodded. "Sure." She felt Molly, who was sitting on her other side, give her knee a supportive squeeze.

She and Eric walked together to the cafeteria door and looked out into the deserted hall. "How 'bout out back?" he suggested, pulling on his faded denim jacket. Katie focused on the jacket and a pang of something like nostalgia tugged at her heart. He wore that jacket all the time — it was as much a part of him, as familiar to her as his eyes, his hair, his smile.

"Out back?" she echoed blankly. "But we're not supposed to go out there during school."

"Well, the quad's too crowded." He took Katie's hand. The gesture made her heart a little lighter. "Let's try it. The worst thing that could happen is we'll get caught, right?"

"Right."

They looked carefully down the hall for any sign of the hall monitor before they ducked into the stairwell. When Eric pushed open the heavy door at the bottom, it gave away with a loud metallic clank. Katie giggled. She felt like a naughty little kid.

Eric glanced at her with a puzzled smile. "What's so funny?"

Katie slipped through the door. It was a cold, cloudy day. There probably wouldn't have been anybody on the quad this lunch period. She crossed her arms and hugged her chest. "Nothing really."

They cut across the lawn behind the school to a path leading into the woods. On any other day Katie would have been swept away by the beauty of the green and gold leaves glowing against the gray sky, but now all she could see was the ground at her feet.

Eric stopped and sat on a fallen tree next to the path. "Katie," he said, putting a hand up to her arm. "Sit down."

She sat down and looked at him with wide, unhappy eyes.

"Katie, tell me I don't have anything to worry about."

When she didn't say anything, he laughed nervously and put an arm around her to give her an awkward hug.

"Last night, you said something was bothering you and I didn't think anything of it," he began. "But then I went to bed and I couldn't sleep. I couldn't get our conversation out of my mind. Something about it just wasn't right." He looked searchingly into her eyes. "It's not like you to keep things from me."

Katie dropped her gaze and fidgeted with a patch coming loose on the knee of her jeans. "I couldn't sleep, either," she admitted.

"So, shoot," Eric urged. "What is it?"

"It's us . . . our relationship." Katie felt the arm around her stiffen. She shivered as if the October day had suddenly grown as cold as December. "I mean, there's nothing really the matter between us," she amended lamely, but her next words only made things worse. "I'm just not sure I'm . . . in love with you the same way anymore."

Eric dropped his arm. It took all of Katie's will to look up and meet his eyes. The hurt and surprise she saw there ripped right through her.

She couldn't bear the heavy silence that had

fallen between them. "Say something!" she begged, her voice cracking.

"Say something!" Eric exploded. He stood up and shoved his fists in his pockets. "What am I supposed to say to that?" He turned his back to her, and Katie heard him take a deep, uneven breath. "Are you going to tell me *why* you feel this way? What did I do wrong?"

Katie jumped up and touched his arm. Eric flinched. "You didn't do anything wrong," she said. Her eyes brimmed over with tears, and she wished she could take back those words about not being in love anymore. She was ready to change her mind, if only Eric would ask her to. She was afraid of losing him, of losing the relationship that had played such an important part in her life for the past six months.

"I didn't mean what I said." She shook his arm gently. "I don't know what I mean. Maybe I need some time, some space, to be by myself and do my own thing."

Katie's words sounded empty even to her. Eric turned toward her sharply. Now he looked more angry than hurt. "Time and space for what? What do you mean, do your own thing?" Something registered in his eyes. "This has to do with crew and Greg Montgomery, doesn't it?" he demanded.

Katie's throat went dry. She had to swallow a few times before she could speak. "Maybe a little . . . but not really. I mean, why should it? I can do crew if I want to."

"Well, something's gotten into you. I told you I didn't think crew was such a good idea." Eric's voice was hard, but Katie could tell he was making an effort to keep it that way. "I don't see where you come off suddenly putting that on top of your list of priorities, anyway."

"I can't believe it!" Katie exclaimed. She angrily wiped at her tears with the back of her hand. "Where do *you* come off telling me what I can and can't do and who I can and can't see?"

"What do you mean who you can see?" he countered. "I didn't know we were talking about *seeing* anybody. Come to think of it, I thought you were seeing *me*. Maybe I was wrong!"

The bitterness in Eric's voice moved Katie, and she struggled to calm herself. "I am seeing you," she said. "But that doesn't mean you own me. I have my own mind and my own life. You of all people should know that."

Eric put a hand up to his face. He rubbed his forehead keeping his eyes covered, but when he removed his hand, Katie could see that his eyes were filled with tears. "I just don't understand, Katie. It sounds like having your own life doesn't leave much room for me anymore."

"It does," she faltered. "It should. I — "

"Either it does or it doesn't," Eric said flatly. His eyes were hard again. "Either you have time for me or you don't. Either you're in love with me or you're not. There's no two ways about it. It's your choice."

"My choice?" Katie echoed. She shook her head dully. All the anger had drained from her body. She just felt weak and cold and resigned.

"Your choice. Me or — or crew." Eric clenched his teeth. "Or should I say, Greg?"

"You know I can't make a decision like that!" Katie heard the frustration and despair in her own voice. "I can't 'choose' between the two of you." She knew, even as she said this, that Eric was right. She had to make a move. "I choose — I choose . . . *me*. I can't put you before everything else, Eric."

Any hurt Eric might have been feeling was veiled by anger. Katie had never heard his voice sound so dark. "I don't know why you're doing this, Katie," he said coldly. "But if you can do without me, just like that, then I can sure do without you."

He turned on his heel and walked away as fast as he could without breaking into a run. He didn't look back.

Katie stood frozen at the edge of the woods behind the high school, hot tears streaming down her face. As she watched Eric's back get smaller and smaller, she felt incredibly small herself. She never thought that she and Eric would break up. She'd never really pictured herself without him. Now that he was gone, Katie realized breaking up was a hundred times more horrible than she could ever have imagined.

Chapter
6

Molly stretched her arms over her head and stood up on her tiptoes, then made her way down the steps to the sidewalk. The cool afternoon breeze lifted the hair from the back of her neck and made her shiver slightly. What a fantastic workout! she thought with satisfaction.

Her aikido class had gone well today. The more she taught, the better she liked it. It was so much fun to turn other people onto karate — kids her age and adults, too. And it was a great way to get in shape, a mental as well as a physical challenge.

She stepped to the edge of the curb and peered down the street. Buses stopped outside the Fitness Center every fifteen minutes or so. She must have just missed one.

Now she reached down and touched her toes, oblivious to the curious stares of people passing her on the sidewalk. She sighed when she straightened up. If only her mind were as serene as her body. She was still thinking about seeing Katie in the hall at school after the last bell that afternoon. Katie had looked like she'd been crying, and Molly felt awful because she hadn't been able to stay and talk. She'd call her first thing when she got home.

The bus rounded the corner and puffed to a stop, exhaust billowing from the rear. Molly swung on and dropped her coins into the fare box. The only empty seat was near the back next to a woman with seven or eight shopping bags, and Molly collapsed into it, practically landing on the woman's lap as the bus pulled abruptly away from the curb. She smiled an apology.

Looking out the window, she watched the wide streets, the lampposts, the stores, and apartment buildings flash by. It was just the kind of gray day that plunged her into a reflective mood. And Katie's problem wasn't the only one Molly was concerned with. She had a problem of her own.

She pressed her nose against the glass like a little kid, almost expecting the woman on the other side to play mother and say, "Don't do that! It's dirty!" She sighed and her breath misted up the window, obscuring her view. I miss Ted, she thought sadly.

She glanced around the bus. Everyone was sitting still, staring straight ahead, looking so alone. Molly wanted to jump up and say, Hey, I know it's hard to be alone. I know how it feels.

She was alone without Ted. Since he had gone, nothing had changed — and everything had changed. She was still here, riding the bus from Georgetown home, down the same streets, looking at the same street lights, passing the same houses, but something was missing in her world.

Molly thought about Greg and Katie. She guessed she could understand how he might want to be with somebody new, now that Chris had graduated. But she didn't want anyone new. She just wanted Ted.

As the bus headed south toward Frederick Avenue, Molly daydreamed about Ted and all the good times they'd shared. She closed her eyes. She could feel the sand under her feet, hear the surf and the screaming of the gulls, smell the salt air. . . . Ted was chasing her down the shore at Ocean City, kissing her on the beach, in the water. . . . Now they were riding the roller coaster at the amusement park, the neon-bright nighttime city sprawled beneath them. . . . Ted was holding her close in the Tunnel of Love. . . .

Molly came back to earth with a jolt. Her stop!

She leaped up, almost landing on the woman again, and scooted through the door just as it was sliding shut. She hit the sidewalk at a run and sprinted all the way home — two blocks down Frederick, right on Sycamore, right on Gleason, fourth apartment on the left. She was going to call Ted and ask him to come home this weekend; maybe her mom would even let her visit him at James Madison!

Inside, the apartment was quiet. Her mother must still be at school. As Molly squeezed into the small kitchen she couldn't help remembering the nice big kitchen they'd had at their old house in Pacific Point before her father died. Oh well, she thought. This apartment really wasn't so bad. It was home, anyway.

She poured a glass of cider and caught her breath before she dialed Ted's number. The phone rang twice before someone picked it up. Ted's voice said, "Hello?" and a smile broke across Molly's face.

"Hi, it's me!" she said brightly. "What's up?"

"What's up? I'm up!" Ted sounded like he was smiling, too. "This is a great surprise! But how come you're calling now when it's so expensive?"

"Oh, I don't know. I guess I missed you." Molly hoisted herself up onto the counter and leaned back against the cupboard, her feet dangling. "And I had a *great* idea! Wanna come home and visit your loving girl friend this weekend?"

"Sorry, Molly. I'm playing football, remember? I've got a game this Saturday! I'll probably just sit on the bench, but I have to be there, anyway."

"Oh." Molly couldn't disguise her disappointment. "So much for my great idea, huh?"

"Hey, don't sound so sad." Ted's voice was affectionate. "You're gonna make me quit the team in a minute. You know I'd love to see you. I'd invite you here but the game's away."

"Well, maybe another time," Molly said with false cheerfulness, determined to be a good sport. "Make a touchdown for me, okay?"

Ted laughed. "If Coach gives me a chance on the field, you've got it."

"Good luck."

"Thanks. I'll call you soon, all right? And Molly, I am sorry this weekend's not going to work out. You know I feel bad about it, don't you?" he asked.

"Yeah, I do," she said honestly.

"I'll be home for fall break after midterms," he reminded her. "That's not that far away."

"I know. I can't wait!" Molly exclaimed. "It'll be great."

"Well, I'll talk to you soon. I . . . I miss you."

The love in Ted's voice made Molly feel warm all over. He cared for her and she cared for him and she realized they had the power to make anything, even being apart, worthwhile.

"I miss you, too. Like crazy. 'Bye, baby," she said softly.

Just as Ted started to say good-bye, there was a knock on his door. "Hold on," he said to Molly before calling, "Come in!"

She heard him greet somebody, one of his new college friends, she supposed. Then a girl's voice answered. The warm feeling deserted Molly as quickly as it had come. She suddenly felt cold and exposed sitting alone on the kitchen counter.

Ted got back on the phone with her. "That's a girl who lives downstairs from me in the dorm," he explained. "Sarah. We have English Comp together and there's a paper due tomorrow. She promised me some ideas."

Molly had to swallow hard to keep from asking questions. She didn't want to sound suspicious. It was only right that Ted should be making new friends. She wouldn't want it to be any other way.

She forced herself to sound happy and unconcerned as she hung up, but she couldn't help putting the phone down with unnecessary force. It was harder to *feel* happy. She didn't like this left-out and jealous sensation — it was new to her.

She hopped down from the counter and shook her head to clear it of those feelings. "This ain't gonna get me down," she said defiantly. Somehow saying it made it more true. "I can have fun on my own, too!"

She crossed to the fridge, opened the door, and studied its contents. Her mother was late. It looked like it was going to be leftovers for dinner again.

The silence of the kitchen pressed down on Molly, and the words she'd just spoken started to seem small and thin. She grabbed the phone and dialed quickly. She needed moral support, and Katie probably did, too. In fact, Katie was probably about a hundred times worse off than she was.

Somehow that thought made Molly feel just a little better. A little guilty, she thought to herself wryly, but definitely a little better.

"Wow," Diana said sympathetically.

"Geez, I'm really sorry, Katie." Elise reached across the glass table top to squeeze Katie's hand.

The girls had met for an emergency ice cream/ rap session at Sticky Fingers. Katie told her story first because it was the worst.

Now she shrugged and stuck her spoon listlessly into her hot fudge sundae. "I'm okay. Really. To tell the truth, I just kind of feel numb right now."

"I know what you mean," Elise assured her.

"When Ben and I first got together, after being friends for so long, and things weren't working out between us, I thought I'd never feel anything ever again." Her dark brown eyes were bright with optimism. "But it'll work out for you and Eric, I just know it."

Katie caught Molly's eye and Molly shook her head slightly. She hadn't said anything to Diana and Elise about Greg. They only knew that Katie and Eric had broken up.

"I'm not sure it will, Elise," Katie said. "It's . . . complicated."

"We'll let Elise think the best," Molly remarked. "Somebody around here's gotta be a hopeless romantic."

Diana sipped at her strawberry milk shake. "Do you *want* to get back together with Eric, Katie?"

"I don't know, Di," Katie answered honestly. "Like I said, when we started talking this afternoon I wasn't planning on breaking up with him, and I know he wasn't planning on breaking up with me. It just sort of *happened*. Maybe it's for the best."

"How can it be for the best?" wondered Elise. "I always thought you two were so perfect for each other." She looked disillusioned.

"Maybe we were," Katie admitted. "I guess I always thought so. We're a lot alike. But remember what you said to me once, Diana. At the beginning, when Eric and I were fighting because neither of us had time to go to the other's meets? You told me that being alike could be just as hard as being different."

Diana nodded. "I remember."

"Well, it really is," Katie said with conviction. "Sometimes being alike doesn't leave you enough room to grow, to be different. Maybe Eric was *perfect* for me, but maybe someday I'll find someone who's *right* for me."

Elise shook her head. "But just last weekend you guys seemed so happy together. You make it sound like you've seen this coming for a long time."

"I definitely didn't *see* it coming, but maybe I *felt* it coming," Katie waved her spoon and attempted a smile. "Whatever, it came, right?"

"Right," Elise pushed back her empty dish. "It's just so . . . *sad*. It's sad to think that can happen to something that starts out so good." Her eyes sparkled from behind a strand of curly brown hair. "In fact, this has got me so depressed that I just gobbled that whole enormous sundae in ten seconds flat."

"Gotten *you* depressed!" Diana exclaimed. "You're not the one who just broke up with her boyfriend."

"I'm sorry, Katie," Elise said contritely. "I didn't mean to be insensitive."

"You weren't," Katie assured her. "Anyway, I feel better when no one makes a fuss over me. It's easier to forget how rotten I *should* be feeling."

Molly gestured with her double-dip mocha fudge swirl cone, and said glumly, "Here, I'll distract you. I'll tell Di and Elise about my conversation with Ted. They haven't heard this one yet."

When Molly finished her story, Elise and Diana

agreed that she had to give Ted the benefit of the doubt. It might not be easy, but it was only fair.

"He's always been honest with you," Katie pointed out through a mouthful of hot fudge and whipped cream. "You can trust him."

"Yeah, but everything's different when you move into the long-distance mode," Molly protested.

Katie knew she was alluding to Greg and Chris. "It doesn't have to be," she argued. "I think if you want it to work, it'll work." Her voice got quiet again. "I guess if I'd really wanted it to work with Eric, I would have tried harder."

Diana polished off her milk shake and caught Molly's eye. "It doesn't look like we did a very good job of cheering you up, Katie." She looked at her watch. "Ooops. It's ten! I told my parents I'd be home by now. C'mon, let's go!"

In the parking lot, Molly and Katie waved good-bye to Diana and Elise and hopped in Katie's car. They were both quiet on the drive home, each lost in her own thoughts. After she dropped Molly off, Katie drove slowly home. Suddenly she was bone-tired. This felt like the longest day she'd ever lived through. She'd broken up with Eric. All she wanted to do now was crawl into bed and fall asleep. She'd have to feel better when she woke up in the morning. She certainly couldn't feel any worse.

When Katie entered the house, her father was watching TV and her mom was in the kitchen emptying the dishwasher. She had told them during dinner about her fight with Eric — it had been all she could do to keep the tears from spilling over and dripping onto her chicken tettrazini. Now she was tired of being brave. She joined her mother by the dishwasher and leaned her head against her shoulder. Mrs. Crawford put an arm around her and patted her hair.

"Are you going to be all right?" she asked gently.

"I'm not sure," Katie sniffled. "It's so hard, Mom."

"I know, honey. I know."

Katie sniffled again, more loudly this time. Maybe being brave wasn't so bad. It beat crying her eyes out. And she had a feeling that if she started crying now, she'd never stop.

She hugged her mother. "I'll be okay, won't I, Mom?"

Mrs. Crawford laughed. "I've never heard that breaking up was fatal."

"Good!" Katie bent over and grabbed a couple of clean plates. "Let me do this. You go watch TV with Dad."

She removed the plates and glasses one by one and placed them in their spots into the cupboard. With every minute that passed she felt a little better. Each spoon and fork put carefully away relieved another bit of tension. When she finally did go to bed, she felt drained but somehow lighter. She fell asleep before she even had a chance to remember she should be crying herself to sleep.

Chapter
7

The rest of the week passed in a blur for Katie. Certain circles at Kennedy were quickly buzzing with the news that she and Eric had broken up. She knew that kind of gossip was inevitable — she took part in it sometimes, too — but nonetheless, she didn't like the feeling that people were looking at her and feeling sorry for her as she walked down the hall. She knew Eric had to be just as uncomfortable as she was.

Actually, she didn't know that. She didn't know anything about Eric right now. He was avoiding her, and she supposed she couldn't blame him. In the cafeteria he sat apart from the gang, eating lunch with some of his swim team buddies. They had history together, but every day he sat at the desk nearest the door and bolted as soon as the bell rang, before she could catch him to let him know she wished things didn't have to be so strained between them.

Katie felt different at school now. She wasn't Eric's girl friend anymore and that sort of made her like a new person. Not that Eric's girl friend had been a bad person to be. A lot of girls at Kennedy would give anything to date him. It suddenly occurred to her that one of these days she might see him around with another girl. It wasn't really a pleasant thought, but she'd set him free so that she could be free — she didn't have any claim on him anymore.

Crew practice was the bright spot in the week. It was more concentrated than her solitary gymnastics workouts, where she had too much opportunity to let her thoughts wander. It felt great to get outside, to let the breeze out on the river sweep her mind clear and make her heart feel lighter. Besides, Greg was there. Katie couldn't pretend that he wasn't most of the reason she was so determined to succeed at coxing, or why she was glad, even though she was also sad, that she and Eric were separated.

She knew Greg had heard about her breakup with Eric, and from the way he looked at her when they were talking about crew, she could tell he was interested. The current between them was warm and electric. At least ten times during practice, Katie found herself thinking about their kiss the other day, and when she caught his eye, she knew he had the same thing on his mind. He was treating her delicately, though. He seemed to be holding off to let her catch her breath and get her thoughts together. This only made her like him better, made the feeling between them more special.

Katie was a little quiet at practice on Friday. Saturday would be the first race she would cox. The butterflies got started in her stomach a good twenty-four hours ahead of time.

When practice was over and the shells had been stored in the boathouse, Greg headed down to join Katie. She was sitting on the dock, looking out at the river. The late afternoon sun touching her hair made it even redder, and the light bouncing off the water turned both their faces golden.

Greg touched her on the shoulder and Katie jumped, looking hastily behind her. "You scared me," she exclaimed. "I thought I was heading for another unexpected swim!"

As he sat down next to her, his sweat pants brushed against her, making her skin tingle. He laughed. "That only happens on the first day of practice. Of course," he added with a sly smile, "then there's the traditional dunking after you win your first *race* and also after you *lose* your first race — "

Katie gave him a playful push. "You're so mean!"

He put an arm around her and hugged her lightly. "Just kidding, K.C. I'll take care of you. You'll stay dry."

"Thanks for nothing."

They sat quietly for a moment, watching the trees on the far side of the river look as though they were catching fire in the glow of the setting sun. Katie was happy. Greg's arm felt good — his nearness excited her, but it also made her feel peaceful inside.

He turned to her and looked into her eyes.

"So, are you ready for Georgetown tomorrow?" he asked solicitously.

Katie shivered inside her big Coca-Cola sweat shirt. "You probably know that better than me!" she said with a wry smile. "I don't *feel* ready. Oh, I hope I don't goof things up for you guys!"

"You won't." He pulled her closer and mussed her hair. "You know how to handle competition. Where's the cool and composed gymnast?"

Katie giggled. "She's still around, but the scared and shaky coxswain is winning out."

Greg shook his head. "I don't believe you. Naw, the Katie Crawford I know's not afraid of anything."

"Well, I guess I should feel fairly confident," she admitted. "I may still be learning, but I have a great teacher and that usually makes the difference."

He laughed. "So now the pressure's on me, huh? Okay, I know what. My philosophy is usually to take it easy the night before a race. Do something fun, do anything but think about crew. But how would you like to come over tonight and watch some crew videotapes? It might not sound very exciting, but it's a good way to pick up some tips on style. And if you pass my crew quiz, maybe we can watch a movie afterward."

Katie narrowed her eyes and pretended to be suspicious. "Are you asking me out on a date?"

Greg shook his head and raised one hand. "Scout's honor! My motives are pure and disinterested!"

Katie looked disappointed and he laughed. "Well, not that pure."

She smiled. "It sounds like fun. When do you want me to come over?"

"Why don't you come over right now? I know my parents would love to have you join us for dinner."

"Thanks, but this is one of my mom's afternoons at Greenpeace. She helps Mrs. Jenkins — you know, Sasha's mother, the woman who owns the Albatross Bookstore — with the local chapter. So I get to cook dinner." She grinned. "I'd invite *you* over, but I wouldn't subject you to one of my casseroles this early on in our friendship!"

He laughed. "Okay. How about eight?"

"I'll be there."

As Katie turned into the driveway of the Montgomerys' house she saw that it was even more impressive up close than it had looked when she dropped Greg off last week. It was enormous, a stately brick Georgian with dark green shutters and a circular drive.

Katie gulped. She felt as if she should be wearing a strapless taffeta cocktail dress instead of a chambray workshirt and a denim miniskirt. Oh, well, too late to speed home and change now, she thought as she parked. She giggled, picturing herself and Greg watching crew videotapes in an evening gown and tuxedo.

She rang the bell. When Greg answered the door himself, she was surprised — she'd expected a butler, or at least a maid.

"Hi, there!" He greeted her with obvious pleasure. Katie was relieved to see he was wearing a pair of beat-up-looking khakis, and socks with holes in the toes, and no shoes. "Come on in."

She glanced up as she stepped through the door. The ceiling of the front hall was probably higher than her whole house. Greg took her jacket and hung it in a walk-in closet at the far end of the hall, saying, "It's just as well you didn't take me up on my invitation to dinner, Katie. It turns out my parents went to dinner and the theater in D.C. with one of my dad's stockholder pals. I ordered in Chinese." He gestured to a wide doorway where Katie imagined the kitchen must be. "There's some left. Want some?"

"No, thanks."

"Well." He took her hand and smiled at her. She smiled back shyly. "Want a tour?"

"Sure!"

"Okay." He looked up the broad, curved, burgundy-carpeted staircase. "Just your basic bedrooms up there." Katie doubted that very much. "Here's the living room." She caught a glimpse of an airy room with a fireplace and French doors, through which the lights of Rose Hill twinkled in the distance. "Kitchen . . . dining room . . . my mom's sitting room . . . and here's the family room."

Katie followed him into a warm, wood-paneled room with a bar at one end. She liked it immediately. It was cozier than the others, more lived-in. He waved her to a big L-shaped couch facing a huge TV screen. When she sat down she sank about a foot into the cushions.

"Soda?" he asked, opening the door of the refrigerator behind the bar.

"Sure, if you have something that's not diet."

78

"You got it."

Greg brought her a Coke and then went to insert a tape into the VCR. "Are you ready to see some of the best coxswains in the business go at it?" he kidded her.

"You bet!"

He settled himself on the couch next to her, and the tape began. Katie knew she should give it all her attention — she could probably learn a lot from it. She'd watched tapes like this to help her with gymnastics, and she'd heard people used them for things like skiing and tennis, too. But with Greg sitting so near her, even though he didn't make any move to touch her, she couldn't concentrate at all. She kept her eyes glued to the screen, but she didn't see anything there.

When it ended, he asked her if it helped. "Um, yeah," she lied hastily. "A lot! I really feel prepared now."

He raised one eyebrow and his upper lip twitched. "It did? You do?"

Katie blushed. "Well, yes."

He lifted his arm and rested it along the top of the couch so that his hand touched her shoulder lightly. "That's funny," he said quietly. "I had a hard time focusing on the TV. You know what I mean?"

Katie twisted a strand of hair around her finger and avoided Greg's eyes. "I guess I do."

"Look at me." He put a hand under her chin and turned her face toward him. "Katie."

"Yes?" She tried to sound cheerful and unconcerned.

"I don't want anything from you. I'm not going to push you. I just want to be with you."

She smiled softly and her eyes were grateful. "Thanks, Greg. That means so much to me."

He leaned forward and kissed her lightly on the cheek. "See. This is easy. We'll take it one step at a time. Okay?"

"Okay."

He jumped up and strode to the TV. "I rented *The Sure Thing* and *Back to the Future*. Hope you like 'em." He rejoined her and this time he put his arm right around her. She snuggled in close.

"Katie," he said in a solemn voice.

She lifted her head to look at him. *"Now* what is it?"

He smiled ruefully. "Sorry! Am I being too serious?"

"I don't mind. What are you thinking?"

He shrugged and fidgeted with one of the buttons on the collar of his oxford shirt. "Maybe I shouldn't ask, but . . . do you want to tell me what happened with you and Eric?"

Katie looked up at Greg and the caring in his eyes made everything suddenly clear to her. "It's okay to ask. A lot of it was you," she admitted her cheeks turning pink. "But I think now that that just stirred up some things that were already there. Like when I wanted to join crew and Eric didn't want me to." There was a touch of bitterness in her laugh. "When we first started going out our problem was we competed with each other too much. But lately I've felt like he was competing *for* me. I think — I think. . . ." Her voice faltered. "I think now that it wouldn't have lasted anyway. Past graduation, I mean."

"Why not?" Greg wondered.

"Oh, we want different things when it comes to college. He's headed one way and I'm headed another."

Greg stretched his legs out in front of him and sighed — an abrupt, dissatisfied sound. "But Katie, have you ever thought about what it would be like to go out with someone younger than you?" He grinned. "I mean, say me, for example. Wouldn't the same thing happen eventually? The going-your-own-way thing?"

Katie shook her head. "Molly and I were just talking about that the other day. Maybe, I don't know. It shouldn't have to." She put her feet on the low coffee table then she lowered them just as quickly, but Greg grabbed them and put them back on the table. She smiled. "Anyway, I thought you said 'one step at a time.'"

He nodded. "Right. Sorry."

They watched the movies and laughed and ate cold Chinese food and talked. Greg walked Katie outside to her car a little after eleven. He kissed her good-night but it was a short kiss. A small step. She drove home feeling lighthearted for the first time in days.

The next morning Katie was jogging in place on the dock. It was cool and she was trying to warm up. She had so much nervous energy inside her she couldn't have stood still if she wanted to.

The Georgetown team was already there, and so were a lot of her friends, Eric excluded. They were planning to watch the crew races, which started at ten, then head back to Kennedy for lunch and the home football game.

Greg looked very official as he bustled around getting everything ready. After the team pep talk he took Katie aside.

"Ready, champ?"

She made a pathetic face. "No. Do I have to do this?"

"Hey, it'll be fun!" He stepped behind her and began gently massaging her shoulders. "You'll be fine. I've never seen anybody, a rower or a cox-swain, learn so fast. It'll be a breeze."

Katie felt herself loosen up, from her shoulders right on down to her toes. Even her mind felt lighter and looser. She *would* be fine. This *was* fun! She wouldn't be doing it otherwise.

"Here, Katie." Katie turned to look back at Greg, who was rooting in an equipment bag on the dock. He straightened up and held something out to her. Katie took it. It was a blue cap with the words *Sally Ride II* stitched across the front.

She looked at him questioningly. "That's the name of my sailboat," Greg explained. He smiled sheepishly. "I've worn that cap in races myself and it's always brought me luck. I hope it does the same for you."

Katie blushed with pleasure. "Thanks, Greg. I know it will."

Before she got in the shell with Greg and the other rowers, Katie squinted up at the bank. Molly intercepted her glance and waved. Well, she couldn't chicken out now. Just about every-body she knew was watching.

It had been months since Katie had competed publicly in gymnastics, but as soon as she was out in the water she felt her heartbeat quicken, felt her entire body become alert, all the telltale signs of being ready to perform.

The race was over before she knew it. Katie hardly heard the cheers from the bank, hardly saw the Georgetown boat drop gradually behind, staying put about a boat's length back. She was only aware of the sounds of the rowers breathing, of the water hissing against the side of the racing shell, of her own voice raised in time to the stroking of the oars. She could feel Greg's strength and intensity flow into her. She didn't realize they'd won until the guys almost tipped the boat in their attempt to congratulate her and one another.

Katie felt a thrill run through her and then a rush of pride and accomplishment. They'd won! She'd done it! It was almost as wonderful as winning at gymnastics!

When they reached the shore, Greg pulled her from the boat and twirled her through the air. "Way to go, K.C.!" he hollered.

"Way to go, Monty!" she shouted back.

He put her down and then lifted her up again to bring her to eye level. He hugged her close. "That was fantastic." He kissed her and she kissed him back. Suddenly she didn't want to take things slow. That wasn't her style, after all. She didn't care if the whole world was watching. The excitement between her and Greg was all that mattered.

After she'd high-fived it with all the other guys on the team, she collapsed on the dock to catch her breath. Greg was giving instructions to the boat who would be racing next. When they won, too, the morning was really complete.

The gang was getting ready to leave the river. Katie ran up the bank to say good-bye while Greg helped Aaron and Carl and the rest of the team members store the equipment. A few minutes later they all headed for the parking lot.

Greg let Katie gush for a full five minutes about how stimulating the race had been, how she'd checked out Georgetown's cox and rowers before the race and could tell they were no match for their team, how she'd known after the first few strokes that they were going to get ahead and stay ahead, and then he silenced her with a long, hard kiss. Katie wrapped her arms around his neck and didn't let go after their lips parted.

"So, what do you say we do something tonight?" Greg suggested in a low, husky voice after the rest of the crew team was long gone.

"I think that's a great idea," she responded, her eyes sparkling.

He brushed his lips against hers and then smiled. "I didn't give you much time to think this falling-in-love stuff over, did I? Sorry." They kissed again.

"I bet you're sorry!" Katie teased.

"So, Miss Crawford — "

"*Ms.* Crawford," she corrected.

"Ms. Crawford, are you ready to let me sweep you off your feet?"

Katie nodded. "Yes, please!"

"What do you want to do? Ben's having a party — "

Team sports were something she was learning to appreciate more at Kennedy.

She glanced at Eric, this time out of the corner of her eye. He didn't *look* as if his heart were broken, but she knew from experience how easy it could be to hide it. She glanced in the other direction. Still no sign of Greg and Katie. Well, it might be for the best, for Eric at least, if they skipped the game today.

Molly had been part of the small crowd at the crew race that morning. To her, the chemistry between Katie and Greg had been very apparent, but then she was the only person who knew something was going on between them. No one else seemed to have noticed their postrace kiss.

She was happy for Katie. Greg was a great guy, and if he was what her friend wanted, far be it for Molly to feel otherwise. But at the same time, she felt terrible for Eric. He was her friend, too, and when she arrived at the football field and found him sitting alone in the bleachers eating a hotdog, she'd realized that maybe he needed her right now even more than Katie did.

He'd just gone back to the concession stand for a giant pretzel and now Molly held her hand out for it. She took a big bite. "Ugh! Mustard?"

"Of course!" Eric said, surprised. "How else would you eat a pretzel?"

"In its natural state, with just the salt it was born with!" She craned her neck. "What was *that?*"

Eric shaded his eyes with one hand. "First and ten. A good sign."

Molly reached for the pretzel again, this time wiping off a little of the mustard with a napkin before taking a bite. The clamor of the enthusiastic fans all around them gave her and Eric a funny sort of privacy. She realized they could talk about just about anything with no one else being any the wiser. She finished chewing and turned to Eric, this time putting her hand awkwardly on his knee.

"Eric," she began in a low voice. He looked at her expectantly, and she could tell by the pained expression in his eyes that he knew what she was going to say. "I — I just want you to know that if you want to talk about . . . anything, I'm here for you."

Eric leaned forward with his elbows on his knees and his chin in his hands, keeping his eyes directed straight ahead, although he didn't seem to be focusing on the game. "Thanks, Molly. That's nice to know."

When he didn't say anything further, Molly turned her gaze back to the game. If he didn't want to talk, he didn't want to talk.

But a minute later, he spoke again, and this time his voice was a little shaky. "It's really hard, Moll."

She patted his shoulder gently, her heart swelling with sympathy. "I know it is. But if I may say so myself, you're holding up pretty well."

He laughed bitterly. "Not without an effort."

Molly let out a deep sigh. "I wish I could say something or do something that would make you feel better, Eric. You just have to give it some time."

"That's one thing I've got now — time!"

Just then the Kennedy quarterback passed for a touchdown and the home bleachers went wild. Molly grabbed a handful of confetti out of the brown paper bag at her feet and threw it at Eric, who'd just opened his mouth to cheer.

"Wahoo!" he sputtered, then grabbed a handful himself to pelt her. Molly burst out laughing.

They settled back in their seats, wiping the confetti off one another's hair and clothing. The tension had been broken, to Molly's relief. Eric seemed more relaxed, too. They watched the game in silence for a while, Eric concentrating on the plays and Molly studying the pictures of the players in the program.

"Hey, he's cute!" she observed to no one in particular. "Wonder why I haven't seen him around before? Oh — a sophomore! Too young for me."

Eric wasn't paying any attention to her. As his next comment demonstrated, he was still thinking about the topic of their pre-touchdown conversation.

"You know, Molly, it's funny," he began. She looked up from the program with a smile, ready for a joke. "In some ways it's not just losing Katie that hurts." Molly's expression grew serious.

Eric looked to their left, and Molly followed his gaze to see Fiona, Jonathan, Elise, Ben, and a few others from their gang. "I suddenly feel kind of out of it all around, you know?" He continued, "I mean, Katie was my original link to that whole crowd. Now I'm not sure I fit in."

Molly sat up straight and slapped her hand on her knees. "Don't be ridiculous!" she exclaimed, her eyes flashing. "That's not true at all. They're your friends now as much as they're hers, and don't you forget it!"

Eric hunched his neck down into the upturned collar of his denim jacket and shrugged. Molly tossed her head. "Well, look at me! Aren't I proof of that?"

He couldn't keep a smile from his lips. "Yeah, Molly, you are," he admitted, ruffling her curls with one hand. "Thanks for reminding me."

"Well, I shouldn't have to remind you," she said, putting on a huffy expression. Then her eyes lit up, becoming twice as blue as usual. "What are you doing tonight, anyway?"

"Um, maybe . . . nothing."

"Wanna go with me to Ben's party, then?" she asked eagerly.

He hesitated and Molly thought she knew why. "Don't worry. Katie won't be there," she said as delicately as she could. "I know for a fact she has other plans."

Eric raised an eyebrow but didn't ask any questions. Molly waited patiently and when he finally nodded, she threw her arms around him and gave him a fierce hug. "I'm so glad! We'll have a blast!"

The game ended up being pretty exciting, even by Molly's standards. Hinsdale tied it up in the fourth quarter, but with three minutes to go, Kennedy scored again on a seventy-yard touchdown run.

When it was all over, Molly stood up and

dusted off the seat of her jeans. She glanced at her watch — only four-thirty. Eric saw the gesture and put an arm around her to pull her in for a possessive hug. "You're not in a hurry to get anywhere, are you? I thought we had a date!"

"But Ben's party won't start until at least nine!" Molly looked at him in surprise, then realized from his smile that he was teasing.

"I'll pick you up around nine, then," he said, stretching his arms so far above his head that his rugby shirt came untucked.

"No, come to think of it" — Molly made a move to tickle him, which he fended off — "I'm not in a hurry to get anywhere. Let's do something now!"

"How about pizza?"

"Pizza?" She shook her head, amazed. "Don't you ever get full?"

"Nope!"

Forty-five minutes later they were sitting at a table at Mario's with Diana and Jeremy, leaning their elbows on the red and white checkered table cloth as they dug into an extra-large pizza with everything on it, except anchovies, at Diana's request. Molly was glad she'd recruited Diana and Jeremy to come along. It took a little of the pressure off her — there were no more chances for a serious talk.

But there didn't seem to be a need for any. Eric was in good spirits and as she watched him tell a funny story, pushing his too-long blond hair off his forehead and turning on that heart-stopping smile, she found herself having serious doubts about her best friend's sanity. How could

Katie break up with a guy like this? The merits of Greg Montgomery aside, Eric was everything a person would be lucky to find in a boyfriend. Fun, adorable, devoted. . . .

She picked a mushroom off her slice and watched as the strand of cheese still connecting it to the pizza stretched longer and longer. Well, she thought, just because Katie no longer wants to spend time with him, there's no reason I shouldn't. This is the most fun I've had in ages!

After they polished off the last crust of pizza and the rest of their pitcher of soda, Diana announced that, believe it or not, she and Jeremy had a dinner date with her parents. She placed a hand delicately over her stomach. "I have an hour and a half to change and get my appetite back!"

Eric laughed. "Good luck!" He turned to Molly. "So what are *we* going to do to work this off?"

She pondered for a minute as they walked out to the parking lot and then grinned mischievously. "I know — the Fantastic Planet!"

"The Fantastic Planet?" he repeated blankly.

"The miniature golf place in Carrolton!" she explained, grabbing his hand and dragging him toward the car. Eric looked back helplessly over his shoulder at Diana and Jeremy. "C'mon, slow-poke," she urged. "It'll be fun!"

Later at the Fantastic Planet, Molly didn't think she had ever laughed so hard. When Eric hit his ball into the little ankle deep pond at the fifth hole and waded into retrieve it, she nearly collapsed. Every hole proved funnier than the last. Then of course, after playing horrendously,

Eric hit a hole-in-one on the last hole and won a free game, so they had to go around the whole thing again.

They stopped for ice cream on the way to Ben's to kill another half hour and arrived at the party at exactly nine. There were already a number of people there and by the time one album was over, the Forrests' living and family rooms were packed.

When Brian Pierson, who had inherited Peter Lacey's noontime show at the high school radio station, WKND, put on one of his crazy new records, Eric grabbed Molly's hand and pulled her over to where a few kids were dancing.

Molly loved to dance, and she wasn't surprised to discover that Eric was a great dancer. To begin with, he was a good athlete and he moved well, and he really opened up on the dance floor. Her boyfriend, Ted, on the other hand was incredibly stiff — a typical, muscle-bound football player, she always teased him.

As they danced, Molly noticed that a few people were looking at them curiously, but she didn't care what they thought. She held Eric's eyes. She could tell he felt a lot better than he had when they first met up that afternoon, and she was glad. Suddenly she realized that she felt a lot better, too. Maybe this "date" tonight wasn't just therapeutic for Eric — maybe she was proving something to herself, too. She was having fun — without Ted. A little tingle of pride at her own self-reliance ran through her.

She was pretty warm by the time the song they were dancing to ended and was about to suggest a road-trip to the refreshments when the next song came on. It was a slower one and instead of letting her go, Eric pulled her closer.

"I've been meaning to tell you, Moll," he said, looking down into her upturned face, "you're great company."

She laughed. "You're no slouch yourself!"

"No, I mean it. This day turned out to be a lot more fun than I expected."

"I'm really glad," she said sincerely.

"One other thing," he continued in a more serious tone. Molly nodded, looking equally solemn. "I'm not exactly tall, but you make me feel like Larry Bird. I get a great view of the freckles on your nose from up here!"

Molly swatted him playfully on the chest. "You clown! I may be short, but I could flip you right here and now if I wanted to." She giggled, remembering the time she and Ted first met and she tried some of her aikido moves on him. Had he ever been surprised!

She giggled again at another thought. "It's funny. Katie always says the same thing, that she doesn't feel so short around me." The minute the words were out of her mouth Molly wished she had swallowed them instead. Katie's name hadn't come up since the football game. And she and Eric were having such a good time, she hated to ruin it now.

She started to apologize but Eric shook his head. "Don't," he said firmly. "It's okay. There's no point in pretending she doesn't exist. I know she's your best friend — do you think I could forget that?"

Molly sighed. "I guess not. I just . . . want you to be comfortable with me, that's all."

He tightened his arms around her. "I am. And thanks." They were silent for a moment before he continued. "Moll, I hope you won't think I'm taking advantage of your position, I mean with me and Katie, but I want to ask you a question."

She shrugged. "What is it?"

Eric took a deep breath. "Is there something going on between Katie and Greg?"

Molly flinched. The last thing she wanted to do was hurt Eric, but he was going to find out sooner or later. It would probably be easier for him to hear it from her than through the grapevine at school. She decided she owed it to him as a friend to be honest. "Oh, Eric," she began in a sorrowful voice.

"It's okay, Moll. You can tell me."

She rested her forehead against his chest. "Yeah, I think something is." She felt his shoulders tense under her hands. "I'm sorry. I don't think she meant to hurt you. She still cares for you. It just . . . happened."

Eric shook his head sharply. "I don't believe things like that 'just happen,' " he snapped. Then he took a deep breath to calm himself. "I shouldn't take this out on you. Sorry, kid."

"Hey, take whatever you want out on me!" Molly gave him a squeeze. "What are friends for?"

The song ended and another one began, still slow. Eric and Molly continued to sway gently together. "I guess I'm not surprised," he continued in a more even tone. "I mean, that there's someone else. It makes the whole thing a little easier to understand. I've been so confused." He sighed. "I suppose I should be mad at Montgomery for stealing my girl friend, huh?"

"Yeah, what do guys do in situations like that?" Molly asked teasingly. "Beat each other up?"

Eric laughed. "Something like that! But it looks like it was at least half her idea." He looked at Molly as if he still hoped she might contradict him.

"I . . . I'm afraid so."

They danced for another minute, and then Eric admitted to Molly that he wasn't hurting quite as much as he did at first. "Every day," he said, "it's a little better. Just a little, but better, you know? I'm starting to believe I'll get over her someday. It'll take a while, but I will."

"I know you will." Molly was encouraging. "No doubt in my mind!"

"And besides," Eric's expression lightened, "all I have to do is look around me to know there are other fish in the sea."

Molly smiled. "*That's* for sure."

He winked at her. "Hey, Molly, remember when you taught lifesaving to the boys' swim team last winter?"

"Sure, why do you ask?"

"Remember what happened when you demonstrated mouth-to-mouth on me?"

She giggled. "Oh, yeah. You were the first model I ever had that kissed me back!"

He gave her a playful squeeze. "I don't remember the procedure very well — maybe I need a refresher course."

Molly looked up into Eric's teasing eyes. He was close to her, very close. She hadn't noticed before how thin the fabric of her long-sleeved T-shirt was. Suddenly she realized exactly what position she was in. She was slow-dancing with Eric Shriver, the extremely attractive swim team captain. It was late in the evening and the room was dimly lit. If it weren't for two things, two things that were pretty hard to forget — that she had a boyfriend and that *he'd* just broken up with her best friend — she would definitely find the situation tempting.

She looked at Eric again. A great smile, gorgeous wavy blond hair, blue eyes to kill for, a fantastic body. . . . The old Molly, the fun-loving California lifeguard, would have thoughtlessly taken a little flirtation like this one a step further, just for fun. And part of her was ready now. Being with Eric like this felt very good. But the other part of her knew that if she did, she might be sorry, on Eric's behalf and on her own.

If she flirted with Eric now, really flirted with him, she'd be using him. Using him to try to prove to herself that she didn't need Ted all that much, that she didn't depend on him, that if he found someone new, she wouldn't be left alone, hurt, and vulnerable.

Molly's gaze was still holding Eric's. The expression in them was playful but innocent. She reached up and gave him a quick peck on the cheek and a warm affectionate smile. Then she rested her head on his shoulder thoughtfully. Danger averted.

Molly sighed. She knew if she was dissatisfied with her situation with Ted, there was nothing to do but confront it — and him — head on. She liked Eric too much to take the risk of hurting him more than he'd been hurt already.

Chapter
9

Between school, gymnastics, crew practice, and Greg, Katie found she didn't have a free minute. Word about her and Greg being a couple had gotten around Kennedy pretty quickly, just as quickly as the news of her breakup with Eric had. At first she felt awkward hanging out with her friends with Greg at her side instead of Eric, but the awkwardness was passing and even though she hated to admit it, the fact that Eric was making himself pretty scarce made it a lot easier for her.

Katie also hated to admit it, but it was hard to feel too badly about Eric, anyway, when she was on cloud nine because of Greg. Cloud nine — make that cloud ninety-nine! He was attentive, affectionate, exciting, and fun: He met her after class or at her locker every chance he got and thought of all the corny, but heart-melting things like flowers and candy. He drew a funny caricature of her coxing the crew team to victory in the Kennedy Invitational Regatta and thumbtacked it to the boathouse wall. They spent time together almost every week night on the premise of doing homework or making October Festival plans, but really all they did was talk and kiss and then talk some more. Katie knew she was getting more involved with him every passing minute, and it was wonderful.

Crew practice had gone well all week, too, and since there wasn't a race that weekend, Katie didn't feel pressured. She could relax and just have a good time. The guys on the team were all a lot of fun, and they made her feel like one of the family right from the start. And as a coach, Greg was fantastic. He didn't play favorites at practice, and she worked as hard as everyone else. When the team had to go for a five-mile run along the river, Katie ran, too. Of course the fact that Greg ran beside her every step of the way made it pretty painless.

Katie looked at her watch. She pulled her hair out of its ponytail and then fluffed up her bangs with her other hand. Five o'clock — quitting time. Greg was sitting cross-legged on the dock with his second boat talking rowing technique. He looked up, saw her watching, and waved, holding up a hand. Five fingers — five minutes.

Katie stuck her hands in the front pocket of her sweat shirt jacket and walked to the far side of the boathouse, whistling as she went. She sat on a narrow patch of grass where she could look out over the river and also, if she craned her neck a little, keep an eye on Greg.

Now she was really relaxed. She leaned back against the still sun-warmed boards of the boathouse, her eyes closed, and Greg's voice a soothing sound in the distance. Then her ears perked up. Somebody was talking nearby.

It sounded like a couple of the guys on the team — Aaron and John maybe? — taking a shell in the door around the corner from where she was sitting. Katie leaned back again and then sat up just as quickly when she realized what and who they were talking about.

One of the voices — she was pretty sure it was Aaron's — said, "Yeah, I was kind of surprised myself. I mean, I thought Kirsten Berg was a fluke. I didn't realize things were so definitely over with Chris, you know?"

"Yeah," the second voice responded. "But it sure looks like he's on the prowl now. Who can blame him, though, huh?"

Aaron laughed. "Right."

This last indirect compliment sailed right over Katie's head. She was still hung up on one word — Chris. What did Aaron mean, he didn't think things were over between Greg and Chris? What was John talking about, saying Greg was "on the prowl?" What did they know that she didn't?

Katie realized she'd forgotten to breathe for a moment. She could tell her eyes were as wide as saucers. She hadn't done anything, but for some reason, she felt as if she'd been caught red-handed.

But what am I guilty of? she wondered, digging up a stone with the toe of her sneaker. Liking Greg when he still likes someone else? But he doesn't still like someone else! she reminded herself. Since that first conversation in the weight room, Greg hadn't even mentioned Chris. And that was because Chris was part of his past and far from his mind, Katie was sure of it.

She jumped to her feet and walked briskly over to the dock. Greg had finished talking to the team, and the guys were taking their oars up to the boathouse and heading for the parking lot. As they walked past her, saying good-bye, Katie couldn't help wondering how many of them were thinking that she was just a victim of Greg's "prowling." She shook her head. Don't be ridiculous! she told herself sternly.

Greg saw her coming. He stood on the dock, his arms crossed over his chest and the corners of his mouth lifted in a smile. When she got closer, he held out his arms to wrap them around her. Katie raised her face for a kiss, and all her worries melted away the instant their lips met. Nothing could be wrong when Greg held her like this.

"This is by far my favorite part of practice," he declared.

"Practice?" Katie said teasingly. "What are you practicing?"

"Kissing you!" He brushed her bangs back and kissed her forehead and then her lips. "It's still new to me. There's a lot I have to learn."

"I don't know. You seem to know the ropes! But let's keep practicing anyway."

Greg rested his forehead against hers so they were rubbing noses. "I think," he whispered softly, "I think I'm falling in love with you. In fact," he added, "I think I've already fallen. I love you, Katie."

Katie didn't need the words as evidence. Any momentary doubts about Greg's feelings had long since disappeared. But hearing him say them for the first time made her feel more special than she'd ever felt in her life. When she echoed his words, she meant it with all her heart.

Greg kept one arm around her shoulders as they walked up the hill to his car. "I really wish I wasn't going away this weekend, K.C. I don't know if I can stand being apart from you!"

She looked up at him in surprise. "Away?"

"I told you, didn't I? I'm going to Boston to see the Head of the Charles. It's the biggest crew event in the country. Hundreds of college, club, and high school boats compete."

"Oh, I remember now," Katie said. "It sounds like a lot of fun."

He nodded. "I'm pretty psyched for it. A bunch of my buddies from sailing camp go to prep school up there — it'll be wild to see them. It means I have a place to stay, too. But I have to admit," he added, grinning, "I'm not quite as psyched to get out of Rose Hill for a weekend as I was a few weeks ago!"

"I'll miss you," Katie said, swallowing her disappointment and smiling as brightly as she could. "I wish I could go, too!"

"I'd bring you if I could. I only have one plane ticket, though."

Katie laughed. "That's okay. And I'll pass on an offer to ride in your duffel bag."

He hugged her. "That's what I like about you, Katie. One of the things I like about you, anyway. You're such a good sport."

"A good sport?" she wrinkled her nose. "Ugh! How unromantic."

Greg grinned. "You know what I mean. I think you're the coolest ever!"

Katie rolled her eyes. "Gee, thanks."

He kissed her softly. "And I can't wait to see you on Monday when I get back." He kissed her again.

"Me, either," Katie said, and meant it.

Well, Katie thought after saying good-bye to Greg. She dumped her jacket and bookbag at the foot of the stairs and then scanned the fridge for a snack. I guess I can survive a weekend without him! I must have done something with my time before we got together.

She found a bowl of onion dip and grabbed a bag of chips from the cupboard. Now that she thought about it, she realized it wasn't such a bad prospect to take a couple of days to herself. It would be a good chance to catch up on her homework — she still had to write up that alfalfa sprouts-that-didn't-sprout for lab — and to work on her gymnastics and spend some time with Molly. She hadn't seen very much of Molly lately, and she felt badly about neglecting her when she must be kind of lonely without Ted.

That was an easy thing to remedy. Katie popped a chip in her mouth and dialed Molly's number on the kitchen phone.

"Hello?" said a bright voice on the other end of the line.

"Hi, Moll! It's me!"

"Hey, Katie! What's doing?"

"Nothing doing. I'm winding down, actually." Katie answered. "Kind of tired after crew. But listen, what are you doing tonight? Do you want to get something to eat at the sub shop and go to a movie or something?"

Molly sounded surprised. "Aren't you going to see Greg?"

"No." Katie told her about his trip to Boston. "But I'd *love* to see you. I know I've kind of been somewhere else lately," she added apologetically.

"I understand," Molly laughed. "But actually, to tell you the truth, I have other plans." She laughed again, in a funny way, Katie thought. "I'm already going to a movie — with Eric."

"Eric?" Katie couldn't hide her shock.

"It doesn't mean anything, Katie," Molly assured her hastily. "We've always been friends, you know that. I've just been seeing him more often the past week or two. I think it helps him to keep busy," she explained.

Katie shook her head, angry at herself. It was crazy to even think for a split second that Molly had any intentions toward Eric. And even if she did, Katie shouldn't care.

Katie forced herself to be open-minded. "That's really nice of you, Moll," she said hesitantly. "I guess he and I are both lucky to have you as a friend, huh?"

"Yeah. Count your blessings!" Molly teased. "So anyway, I just called him and invited him to the movies, so he wouldn't sit home tonight and mope."

Katie plunged in. "How's he — how's he doing, anyway?"

"Pretty well," Molly said. "He doesn't have any hard feelings, Katie," she added gently. "He'll be okay."

"I'm glad."

"And guess what I'm doing tomorrow?!" Molly's voice grew excited. "I'm taking the train to surprise Ted at school!"

"Fantastic!" Katie exclaimed. "Oh, Molly, that's a great idea. He'll be so happy!"

"I sure hope so! I'm staying over Saturday night with my cousin, Alison. Ted and I can spend two whole days together. I think that's a lot to be happy about."

"I'm sure he'll agree. Well, have fun tonight with. . . ." Katie faltered. "And have a great trip! Give my love to Ted!"

"Will do. I'll call you when I get back."

"See ya!"

Katie hung up the phone and sighed. Molly's news that she had a date with Eric had unsettled her at first. She'd never doubted that Molly was a good friend, though, and her paying special attention to Eric's feelings simply proved it.

But still . . . Katie scooped up some dip with a potato chip and munched it pensively. Thinking about Molly and Eric at the movies together reminded her of all the movies *she'd* seen with Eric. She couldn't help feeling a little out in the cold. If only there was someone else she could call — the prospect of spending the evening alone with nobody to talk to besides her family was suddenly very depressing. But Elise and Diana had dates, too.

Katie pushed the dip away sadly. Then Greg came to her mind, and soon she found herself glowing again. How could she feel sorry for herself when she was in love with the greatest guy in the world? She smiled and did a little gymnastics-style bounce off the kitchen floor. She would have done a back handspring if there'd been any room. She'd have a good weekend, and then she'd be with Greg again on Monday. She couldn't wait.

Chapter
10

Molly took a taxi from the train station to James Madison University after her two-hour ride south to Harrisonburg, Virginia. She didn't trust herself to get on a bus going in the right direction. Once inside the cab she rolled down the window and let the crisp October breeze ruffle her hair. It couldn't have been a more gorgeous day. The sunshine was blinding, but not too bright to dim the brilliant colors of the passing trees.

She got out of the cab as soon as they were on campus. She wanted to experience Ted's new home as fully as she could, so she planned to walk to the football field, exploring as she went. It was such a beautiful place! Some of the buildings were brick, some were old gray stone, all were touched with crimson and yellow ivy. Everywhere, kids were walking, or rather men and women, Molly thought to herself. They all looked so *old*, at least a lot older than she did. The girls were wearing the latest fashions, and the guys looked as if they shaved more than once or twice a week like most of her guy friends at Kennedy did.

She kicked through a pile of leaves on the sidewalk. For the first time she felt sort of excited herself at the prospect of going to college. She'd never really given it much thought before. She'd always lived from year to year, summer to summer, but now she pictured herself two or three years from now, safely embarked on a college career someplace like this. Looking older and feeling older.

It wasn't hard to find the football field — it was where everyone was headed. Molly took a seat on the home team side just in time for kickoff. She'd bought a program when she paid for her ticket at the gate, and now she quickly found Ted's name on the roster. All the James Madison players looked alike from here, especially with their helmets on. But as soon as she picked out Ted sitting on the bench, she wondered how she could have had trouble spotting him. The set of his broad shoulders — even with pads on — was so familiar, and the wisps of light brown hair that curled out from underneath the back of his football helmet brought a smile to her lips.

Molly looked around casually. She was surrounded by sophisticated students, none of whom had to look in the program to identify players. She was sure she stood out like a sore thumb, obviously someone's little sister or, worse still, somebody's still-in-high-school girl friend up for a visit.

Oh well! she thought, her enthusiasm undampened. None of these people care who I am. All that matters is, I'm here!

Pretty soon she forgot to be intimidated. The game was too exciting. When Ted went in for the starting quarterback in the fourth quarter, she cheered so energetically she almost fell off her seat. It was a close game, too, but James Madison held off a touchdown threat in the last few minutes and won, 28 – 17.

Molly couldn't wait to see Ted's face when she ran onto the field and surprised him. The game couldn't have ended fast enough for her. Now she wove her way through the dispersing crowd, the smile on her face growing wider with every step. Other players stood in groups with their families and girl friends. Soon she could see Ted. One of his teammates was swatting him on the back, clearly congratulating him on a well-played game. Molly's heart swelled with pride.

She broke into a trot and came into Ted's field of vision just as he was taking off his helmet and shaking out his damp hair.

"Hey, Mason!" she called out. "Great game!"

Ted stared at her for a full three seconds — it felt like three hours to Molly — before a hint of recognition spread over his face. He smiled. It wasn't exactly the overjoyed smile she was expecting, however. There was something about it that wasn't quite wholehearted.

He held out his arms for a hug, though, and

110

she jumped into them, throwing her arms around his neck and planting a big kiss on his mouth.

"Molly, what are you *doing* here?" he exclaimed, shaking his head in amazement.

"Surprising you — what does it look like?" she teased.

"Well . . . I am surprised, that's for sure!" Ted pressed Molly against his chest, or rather against the pads under his uniform. She kissed him again, and this time she couldn't help noticing that he wasn't very responsive. She hoped it was only because he was tired after a hard game. What else could it be? she thought.

"This is okay? Isn't it? You're happy to see me?" Molly looked straight into his blue eyes, her own eyes wide.

"Of course," Ted said slowly. Then he nodded his head and grinned. "Of course!"

"Good!" Molly stepped away from Ted and looked around her at all the people bustling on to and off the field. "So what do we do now?"

"First," Ted said, untucking his football jersey and flapping it to air himself. "I go to the locker room."

"Where do I go?"

He shrugged. "How about meeting me at the gate over there in about ten minutes?"

"Okay! Sounds good!" Molly waited for Ted to head in that direction, assuming he'd walk her to the gate before going to the lockers. To her surprise, he started off without another glance at her.

"I'll be right out!" he called back over his shoulder, breaking into a jog.

"Sure," Molly said, more to herself than to anyone else.

She put her hands in the pockets of her oversized black and white jacket and pushed them down deep, then turned on her heel and started slowly for the archway that led to the rest of the campus. To say that she felt like a popped balloon was putting it mildly. Be fair, she advised herself. If you'd just played football and were still in a grubby uniform, you'd be dying to strip off your clothes and jump in the shower, too.

On the other hand, if Ted had walked up to you after you had just played a strenuous game and won, all you'd care about would be seeing him.

Molly willed herself to stop thinking such negative thoughts and let the words, "It's going to be a wonderful weekend" run over and over in her mind. When she finally convinced herself that Ted had hurried off to shower so he could come back to her all the sooner, she was able to relax a bit.

She tossed her weekend bag onto the grass on the near side of the gate and looked at the clock on the scoreboard. In five minutes, Ted would be with her and everything would be fine. The afternoon would start fresh.

Ten minutes later she glanced at the clock again. He was taking longer than he'd said he would. She took her compact mirror and hairbrush out of her purse and gave herself a quick going over. She wanted to look her best. Ted had to find her irresistible.

Another five minutes passed, and Molly jumped

restlessly to her feet. She knew it really wasn't a big deal, but she felt anxious, anyway. She put her hand up to her eyes and peered in the direction of the locker room. A bunch of kids were standing outside the door — a few guys and a few girls with a big cooler. They looked like they were ready to start partying.

Just then Ted emerged, his wet hair slicked back. As Molly watched, one of the girls — she was tall with swingy, dark blonde hair — stepped apart from the others to stand very close to him. The girl said something and Ted laughed as he answered, then gestured in Molly's direction.

Molly shrank down inside her jacket, wishing she were invisible. The blonde girl glanced her way briefly before turning back to the rest of the group. Ted waved good-bye to them and started for the gate.

He joined Molly and picked up her bag to carry it for her, and they walked under the archway together. He didn't put his arm around her or touch her in any way, and Molly had to bite her lip. It didn't mean anything, she thought. But Ted was usually so demonstrative. It might not mean anything, but it sure left her feeling cold.

"Who were those people?" Molly asked, hoping she sounded curious rather than suspicious.

"Oh, friends from the dorm." Ted waved a hand dismissively. "We'll probably bump into them later."

Molly bit her tongue this time. She wanted to ask, "Why didn't you introduce me to them? Was that Sarah from downstairs?" but she restrained herself. She had to give Ted a chance to share

113

his new life with her. She couldn't force it.

But as they walked on — to the post office and the snackbar because Ted was starving and he also wanted to check his mail — Molly waited in vain for him to start talking, *really* talking to her.

When Ted stopped in front of a bulletin board in the P.O. to check a sign labeled MIDTERM EXAM SCHEDULE, it occurred to Molly for the first time that maybe her timing in coming up to surprise him wasn't exactly ideal. "Midterms?" she asked, looking up with him at the schedule. "You have midterms? When?"

"In another week," Ted said. He concentrated on the sheet and spoke out loud to himself. "Chemistry, Tuesday at two, Government, Wednesday; at nine. . . ."

Molly gulped. Ted didn't sound too happy. Although who was ever happy about having exams? "So I guess you have a lot of studying to do, huh?" she observed lamely.

"Yeah. I was pretty much planning to spend the whole weekend in the library."

"Oh," was all Molly could think to say in answer to that. Ted might as well have come right out and said that she was going to be in the way, that he didn't want her there. His tone didn't leave a lot to the imagination.

As they headed upstairs to the snackbar to buy sodas and chips, Molly couldn't resist asking one question. "Do you have a midterm in English?"

"Yep." Ted stuck some coins in a vending machine and pulled out a packet of M&M's. "Another paper to write, a longer one this time. Want some?"

"No, thanks." Another paper, Molly thought. He and Sarah were probably working on it together! She sighed.

In a few minutes they were standing in front of Ted's dorm. He took her hand as they walked up the steps and for a moment, Molly's heavy heart lightened. Once they were alone in his room, everything would be fine. Ted would kiss her and say all the things he might not feel comfortable saying out in public here at his new school.

"Wow, this is great!" Molly exclaimed enthusiastically as she entered the room. She looked around and nodded with approval. It was kind of cluttered — two desks and two chairs, overflowing bookshelves, a stereo and an extensive record collection, typewriters, plants, and posters — but very collegiate, she thought. It was exactly what she'd imagined a college student's room would look like. And it was all Ted's! She was awestruck.

Through an open door she could see the bedroom Ted shared with his roommate, Kent Blackburn. She turned to Ted and gestured at the bedroom with her bag. "I feel kind of overdressed. I think I'll just change into jeans and a sweater. Can I use your room?"

"Sure. Make yourself at home," he said lightly.

She went into the bedroom and took off her jacket, then looked back shyly at Ted. He laughed as she closed the door between them.

Molly stepped out of her black tube skirt and pulled on a pair of very faded jeans. Definitely an improvement — she felt more relaxed already.

Glancing around the bedroom, she was able to pick out some of Ted's possessions, little things that made her feel as if she were in his room at home in Rose Hill. His high school letter jacket slung over the post of the bunkbed, a poster of Joe Montana, the stuffed bear they'd won together at the amusement park last summer, a picture of her, her hair tousled and wet, at the beach in Ocean City.

She smiled as she started to pull her heavy white Shaker knit sweater over her head and then she stopped, her arms still raised. She could hear Ted's voice through the closed door. He was talking quietly, but she could hear him.

She stood as still as she could and listened but she couldn't distinguish the words. A few seconds later there was a clatter as Ted hung up the phone.

Molly drew her sweater down over her waist, her heart pounding. She might not have heard the words, but it was pretty obvious what Ted must have been saying and who he must have been talking to. It must have been a girl — maybe that Sarah. There was no other reason for him to be so secretive! Maybe he'd had a date that night and was calling to cancel it. A date to write their final English paper, Molly thought, not sure if she was more upset or more disgusted.

She'd clearly ruined everything by surprising him this way; she'd disturbed all his carefully made plans. He'd been trying to get that message across to her ever since he first saw her and now he'd finally succeeded. Well, he didn't have to put up with her. She'd planned to stay overnight in her cousin's dorm, but now she had no desire to. She wasn't going to hang around where she wasn't wanted.

Molly slipped her feet back into her boots and took a deep breath. She had to look composed. As she opened the door, she plastered a big, insincere smile across her face. Ted turned away from his desk where he was shuffling a stack of papers.

"Ted!" she exclaimed, hitting the palm of her hand to her forehead. "You'll never believe what I just this minute remembered! I have to teach an aikido class tomorrow morning. At nine o'clock." She rolled her eyes and hoped she looked rueful rather than on the verge of tears. "I guess I'd better take a train home tonight, huh?"

The excuse sounded feeble and Molly half expected Ted to laugh it off as a joke, or if he believed her, tell her they'd call the Fitness Center in the morning saying she was sick. But he didn't. He looked around and sounded regretful as he said, "Gee Molly, I'm really sorry. I was looking forward to spending the whole weekend with you," but he didn't look or sound regretful enough. He didn't try to persuade her to stay, threaten to hold her prisoner. It was clear she couldn't leave soon enough for his taste.

Looking at a schedule he'd taken from his desk drawer, Ted found a train that left in half an hour. "Just enough time to stop at the ice-cream shop on the way to the station," he said lightly.

Ice cream was one of Ted's all-time favorite things, as Molly well knew. She was darned if she was going to do anything to make him happy when he'd done a good job all afternoon to make her miserable. "I'm not really hungry," she said as she climbed into the passenger seat of his red MG. "Let's skip the ice cream."

"Whatever you say, Moll." Ted sounded as if he didn't have a care in the world. Molly could have slapped him for being so nonchalant. Instead she just clammed up. They didn't say another word to one another the entire way to the train station.

When they pulled up in front, Ted shifted into neutral. He's not even going to park the car and walk me in! Molly thought, astonished. It was the final insult. He'd probably just shake her hand good-bye.

He gave her a hug, however, pulling her close and pressing her head to his shoulder. "I'm sorry, Molly," he began, stroking her hair gently. Molly suddenly felt a spark of hope. He'd apologize for treating her badly and promise to make it all up to her if she'd only stay the weekend.

"I'm sorry if I've been kind of distracted," he continued. "It's just . . . college life, you know?"

"Right," Molly answered, not caring if her voice gave away her bitterness. They kissed quickly and she walked into the station, her bag slung over one shoulder.

College life, she thought a few minutes later as she gazed dully out of the train window at the lights of the passing towns. College life. It's pretty obvious Molly Ramirez doesn't fit into that scheme anywhere.

Chapter
11

Katie waited at her locker a full ten minutes on Monday afternoon before giving up on Greg. It was strange — lately she'd been seeing him a dozen times during the course of a school day and today she hadn't bumped into him once. He hadn't met her between classes, she didn't see him at lunch, and he wasn't here now. It was definitely strange, and it was very disappointing. She'd missed him so much over the weekend and was really looking forward to welcoming him back from Boston.

When she finally walked out to the parking lot she looked for his mom's white Mercedes, but it was nowhere in sight. She drove home slowly, turning the heat on in her car for the first time all fall — it was a cold day — wondering why she hadn't seen or heard from Greg. Now that she thought about it, it was a little surprising he hadn't called her last night as soon as he got home. *She* would have called *him* if the roles were reversed. And there was no crew practice today either — they wouldn't be together there.

She toyed with the idea of swinging by Greg's house but decided against it. Even though she was sure of his feelings for her, it was still early in their relationship. She didn't want to be pushy. She'd just go home. He'd be sure to call.

The phone was ringing as Katie unlocked the front door. She dropped everything she was carrying on the steps to fumble with the key and then tripped over the vacuum cleaner on her way into the kitchen. She grabbed the phone on the sixth ring and shouted hello. It was Molly.

"Are you okay, Katie? You sound frantic!"

"Oh, I was just running an obstacle course through my house," Katie panted. "What's up?"

"Well, I just got home, and I really don't feel like sitting around alone all afternoon feeling sorry for myself," Molly explained. "Wanna go pumpkin shopping at that farm stand out on the highway?"

Katie had spoken with Molly after she'd gotten back from her disastrous "weekend" with Ted. She knew her friend was making a big attempt at keeping her chin up. Molly needed all Katie's support and it wouldn't be very considerate if she put her off just because she wanted to sit by the phone in case Greg called.

"To tell you the truth, Moll," she admitted, "Greg's supposed to call any minute now." He *would* be calling any minute, she thought, so that really was the truth. "But I want to see you. Why don't you come over here and hang out with me?"

"How about I pick up a pumpkin on my way over? We can carve it at your house."

"Sounds good! See you in a while."

When Greg didn't call during the next half hour, Katie decided he must be jogging or working out. When he didn't call in the hour it took Katie and Molly to carve a face on the pumpkin — it looked exactly like Jonathan Preston, they realized with much giggling — and to rehash Molly's visit with Ted (Katie offered Molly both a "this is the end of the line" observation and a "give him the benefit of the doubt" analysis), Katie couldn't restrain herself any longer.

"Molly!" she burst out as they stood by the kitchen stove making hot chocolate. "I'm going crazy. It's five o'clock and Greg still hasn't called!"

Molly wrinkled her freckled nose. "So?"

"I mean, he hasn't even called since he got home from that Head of the Charles thing! What do you think that means?"

Molly narrowed her eyes slyly. "Do you want an optimistic or a pessimistic analysis?" she teased. When Katie frowned she added lightly, "Look, it's probably no big deal. He's probably waiting for *you* to call."

Katie perked up. "You're right! I bet that's it." She poured the hot chocolate into two mugs and took the whipped cream from the fridge. Shaking the can, she pointed it threateningly at Molly. "If he doesn't call by dinner, *I'll* call *him*."

Molly raised her hands in mock surrender. "Don't shoot! I support you all the way!"

Katie grinned. Handing Molly a mug, she proposed a toast. "Here's to the 'best case' scenario every time!"

At six o'clock Katie waved Molly out the door and then picked up the phone to dial Greg's number. He answered the phone and her heart skipped a beat. "Hi, there!" she said cheerfully. "Guess who? It's somebody who's really missed you. How was your weekend?"

"Oh, hi, K.C." The words fell heavily on Katie's ears. Greg's voice didn't echo her own eagerness but rather was cool and distant. He sounded as if he were still in Boston or even farther away. "It was fine."

"Oh," Katie said, momentarily thrown. Then she collected herself. "Well, I'd love to get together. It's been *days*! Do you want to come over after dinner and have dessert with my family? My mom made an apple pie."

"I don't think . . ." Greg began. He cleared his throat and started again. "Um, thanks anyway, but . . . I'll come by around eight to pick you up. We'll go for a drive, okay?"

"Okay. If that's what you want." Katie tried to sound breezy. It was an effort not to ask him why he hadn't phoned her earlier. "See you then!"

"Yep! 'Bye."

She hung up the phone, slightly unsettled. She had faith in Greg and in the "best case" theory, but something told her that everything wasn't quite as it should be. Well, she thought as she grabbed a handful of silverware and placemats and began setting the table, I'll find out in a couple of hours.

Greg hung up the phone at his house feeling determined but miserable. Katie had been so happy — he hated to hear the disappointment creep into her voice and know that he was the one who'd caused it. And that was nothing, he thought grimly. Wait until tonight!

He pushed the phone aside with his toe and rested his feet on the coffee table with a deep sigh. He hadn't said anything to her about it yet, but his weekend hadn't gone at all like he'd expected. He didn't remember much about the rowing although he knew he could safely assume there'd been some great racing. He supposed he'd had fun with his sailing camp buddies. There was only one thing that stuck clearly in his mind about the whole forty-eight hours. He'd seen Chris.

He wished he could stop thinking about it, but the scene kept flashing over and over in his head, instant replay style. It wasn't that seeing her made him want to be with her again, although she had looked beautiful. In fact, he couldn't recall ever seeing her look better. Her soft blonde hair was longer, her cheeks were pink from the crisp New England fall air, there was something different about her, something intangible. She seemed older, more exciting. And she was happy — maybe that was what made her sparkle. She'd come to Cambridge just for the day with friends from college, and she really seemed to belong in the group and in the whole college scene, even more than she'd belonged to her old crowd at Kennedy.

It had felt good to see Chris, but it had felt just as right to say good-bye to her when the time came to head in different directions. No, Chris didn't inspire any longings in him anymore. But talking to her, studying her familiar face, hugging her before they parted did bring back memories, not just happy ones. It reminded Greg of how much it had hurt when she went away to college, how difficult it had been to accept the fact that she was moving on and he was left behind to start over as best he could. Somehow this meeting had stirred up more feelings in him than the one they'd had a month ago at home in Rose Hill when they'd agreed that their relationship was really over for good.

For good. Maybe it *would* all work out for the best, Greg conceded to himself, staring at the hole in the toe of the rag sock on his right foot. After all, he was falling in love with Katie. But it had hurt. It still hurt. And Katie was a senior now, just like Chris was last year, while he was still only a junior. If he got close to Katie, in the spring it would just happen all over again.

Greg jumped to his feet and flipped on the TV, then the VCR. He stuck in the nearest tape and waited for the movie to begin. When it did, he realized it was *Attack of the Killer Tomatoes*, the movie he'd seen at the drive-in on his very first date with Chris. Afterward, he'd sentimentally gone to the video store to buy it, thinking he'd want it forever as a memento of their falling in love.

He ripped the tape out of the machine and hurled it against the wall, clenching his teeth. Then he buried his head in his hands. He couldn't bear to be hurt like that again. It was better not even to start something new. Not with Katie, who was a year older than he was. Not with sweet, adorable Katie, who Greg had a feeling he could come to care for more than he'd ever cared for anyone.

Katie ransacked her drawers, searching for her pearl-gray sweater dress. T-shirts and sweaters went flying. A pair of wool leggings were draped over a lamp and a miniskirt dangled from her bed post. It was 7:55, and she'd already changed her clothes four times since dinner.

She whipped the dress over her head and fluffed her hair with her fingers as she checked out her reflection in the full-length mirror. She focused on the neckline of the dress — it needed *something*. Pearls? Too dressy. Her jade necklace and earrings? Perfect!

Ordinarily she wouldn't go to nearly so much trouble just for a drive — she was definitely the blue jeans and T-shirt type — but tonight she wanted to look nice. She didn't go so far as to admit to herself that deep inside she had a feeling she was going to need the moral support of knowing she looked her best.

The doorbell rang and Katie bolted down the stairs, coat over her arm. She wanted to head Greg right back out to his car before her parents, or worse still her younger brothers, intercepted him.

She opened the door and stepped outside just as Greg was raising his hand to ring the bell again. "Hi, there!" she greeted him, standing on her tiptoes for a kiss. She expected him to bundle her in his arms for a real smooch. Instead he gave her a quick peck and turned on his heel, taking her hand briskly as he did so.

"I'm so glad to see you!" she tried again as she hopped into the Mercedes. "It feels like forever since Friday, doesn't it?"

Greg nodded and started the engine without a word. Katie laughed. He was teasing her — that was it! Just pretending to be serious to see if he could get a rise from her. Well, she'd give him one! She wiggled her hands under the waist of his jacket and started tickling him. "Come on, Monty!" she cajoled. "Don't be so mean. Crack a smile!"

She felt his body tense under her hands and she stopped in mid-tickle. The blank expression on his face when he turned toward her caused her to pull back completely and sink down into the passenger seat. His eyes weren't warm and teasing. Instead of being the color of a sunlit ocean they were clouded over and gray. And he wasn't smiling. When he did speak it was only to say, "Katie, I need to talk to you."

Her heart contracted. "About what?"

He checked the rearview mirror and then pulled out into the left lane to gun the Mercedes around the car in front of them. He was driving much too fast. "How about dessert at the Bistro Français?" he suggested, not answering her question.

"Fine," Katie said in a small voice. The Bistro was an elegant little French cafe — very romantic, and their pastries were famous. But suddenly she'd lost her appetite. In fact, she felt a little ill.

126

She turned hopefully to Greg. She had to be imagining his coldness. This wasn't the Greg she knew. Greg was open and affectionate and entertaining. The person sitting next to her in the car tonight might as well have been a stranger to Katie. The more she concentrated on the hard lines of his profile the less familiar it looked and the more she wondered how well she actually knew Greg Montgomery.

They drove a mile or so in uncomfortable silence. Katie swallowed. She couldn't stand it. She'd loosen him up if it killed her. "So," she said in her most bubbly manner, "you haven't told me anything about your weekend in Boston! Was the crew stuff pretty neat?"

"Yep."

"How was the weather? Colder than it is down here?"

"Yeah."

"I bet those races inspired you to row like crazy yourself the rest of the season."

"Uh-huh."

Katie turned away from him sharply, digging the fingernails of her right hand into the armrest. Out the window she saw the lights of the Bistro Français. They were pulling into the parking lot.

This is absurd, she thought, feeling her breath coming faster. She'd get more of a response talking to her stuffed Paddington! She and Greg were supposed to be two people in love, not opponents in a chess match. She glanced his way. She could almost see the tension vibrating in the air between them. A scene was coming, she knew it, and she wasn't planning on having one in a booth in the Bistro, no matter how dark and secluded it might be. It wasn't her style to keep things inside. Greg's old girl friend might have been known as the ice princess of Kennedy High, but not her. No sir, Katie thought. When she got steamed, nothing could stop her from boiling over. And she was burning now.

Greg had parked the car and was about to open his door when Katie whirled on him, her eyes sparkling with angry, confused tears. "Do you mind," she said, her voice shaking with emotion, "do you mind telling me why you're treating me like this?"

Greg took a deep breath and gripped the steering wheel so tightly his knuckles went white. He turned to Katie, his eyes managing to look both incredibly blank and incredibly pained. Katie held his gaze, a strange calm stealing over her. How bad could what he had to say to her really be?

"I saw Chris in Cambridge," he began in a low, uneven voice. Katie shook her head disbelievingly. "Katie . . . Katie, I just don't know if I can get involved with you. I — "

Before Greg could finish, Katie was fumbling with the door handle. His words had torn right through her, leaving a harsh ache around her heart. This was absolutely the last thing she'd expected. She never thought she would hear him say things were over. And because he wanted to get back together with Chris!

"Katie, listen," he started to say, grabbing her

arm just as she managed to wrench the car door open and place one foot on the pavement.

"No, you listen to me!" she sobbed, flinging his hand from her arm with a violent gesture. "I can't believe you! I can't believe you would lead me on like this" — her voice caught. It was hard to get the words out through her tears. " — pretending to be free for me, using me, when the whole time you were still in love with Chris!"

"Katie!" Greg reached for her again, shaking his head vehemently. "That's not — "

"Don't touch me!" she exclaimed, shoving his hands aside. "And don't talk to me! I don't want to hear any more of your lies. It's just fine with me if you and Chris are back together, just fine. Because I never want to see you again!"

Katie scrambled from the car, slamming the door so hard behind her it drowned out whatever Greg might be saying. She started running across the parking lot. She heard a crash as Greg flung open his own door and hit the car parked next to his. Then he was calling to her, his voice desperate. "Katie, come back! You don't understand!" But she didn't stop.

When the heel of her pump caught in a crack in the pavement and her foot pulled free, Katie had to turn around for a second to retrieve her shoe. She could see Greg standing by the car, his shoulders slumped. He sounded far away now, his words thinner, weaker. "Katie, please. Stop."

She shoved her foot back in the shoe and raced around the corner onto Rose Hill Boulevard just in time to flag down a bus and jump on.

Chapter
12

"I tell you, Molly, I am ready to swear off boys forever. I'm not kidding!"

Katie and Molly sat on a bench in the near-deserted quad, their jacket collars turned up against the brisk fall breeze and their lunch bags open beside them.

Molly patted Katie's shoulder consolingly. "I can relate, I really can," she assured her friend. She stuffed a very large potato chip in her mouth before adding, with a crunch, "I'm all for putting both Ted and Greg in one of those stupid crew boats without an oar and shipping them out to sea!"

Katie laughed grimly. "Count me in on the bon voyage party!"

"We'll call the boat something corny and tragic like *Lost Dreams* or *Broken Hearts*," Molly suggested. "You can christen it."

"Gee, thanks." Katie pulled a pear out of her

lunch bag and then crumpled the brown paper into a ball. She sighed, her expression suddenly very sad. "It's just so discouraging, you know?" she said. "I mean, last year when I started seeing Eric I was so happy to finally have a boyfriend. I always thought I was missing something. It was such a great feeling to have a guy — a cute one, too — like me back! I'd had so many dumb crushes that never worked out. Remember?"

"Remember?" Molly hooted. "How could I forget? Every week it was someone new!"

"No it wasn't!" Katie defended herself. She shot a sly glance at Molly through her bangs. "Did I ever tell you I had a crush on Ted once, ages before you moved to Rose Hill?"

"No way! That's a scream. What happened?"

"Absolutely nothing." Katie turned her head away and delicately spat out a pear seed. "He didn't even know I existed! It was definitely the old I-might-as-well-be-invisible syndrome."

Molly struck a glamorous pose and fluttered her eyelashes. "I guess he knew somebody incredibly special was about to walk into his life. He was blind to anyone else."

Katie rolled her eyes. "That must have been it. But anyway, being a couple wasn't as easy as I thought it would be. Things were so rocky with Eric at first, with all our competition about our sports and stuff. And then we broke up . . . and now this, with Greg." Katie sighed deeply. "It isn't fair."

"It isn't," Molly agreed. "Nothing's fair when it comes to a relationship. You've just got to give it your best shot. You can't do anything more."

"But I did give Greg my best shot," Katie protested, kicking morosely at a tuft of grass with the toe of her cowboy boot. "Everything was fine. I thought we were in love, really in love. Boy, was I fooled!"

Molly shook her head. "Maybe. It's hard to believe, though. Greg's such an up-front guy. Are you sure you're not misreading him?"

"Misreading him?" Katie snorted. "He practically said, 'I'm getting back together with my old girl friend'. He just doesn't have the guts to say it to me straight out."

Molly shrugged. "I guess there's nothing you can do about that."

They finished their lunches without talking, then spread their jackets on the grass and lay down with their faces to the sun. Molly put her arms behind her head and sighed. "Won't be able to do this for much longer," she observed. "Summer is already starting to seem like a long-ago memory."

"I know." Katie turned her head to look at Molly. For her, summer had been Eric, and thinking about it, and him, made her sad. "Moll," she began, swallowing the tears that were tickling her throat, "do you think I was a fool for breaking up with Eric? We had something good, didn't we?"

Molly was silent for a moment. Katie could see her furrowing her brow. "Yeah, of course you had something good. You never doubted *that*. The point was that you found something better, for you, anyhow. Right?"

"I thought so," Katie said slowly. A tight feeling in her throat let her know tears were threateningly close. She sniffled. "No, you're right. Even if I was only with Greg for a really short time, it was worth everything I gave it to feel what I felt when we were together. It was really special."

Molly turned her face away. "You're lucky, then."

"Maybe I am. I don't feel too lucky right now, though. I just feel lonely. All I have left are memories. I've lost Eric *and* Greg."

Katie rubbed her eyes, streaking tears across her cheeks. Molly hitched herself up on one elbow and reached the other arm out to give her friend a hug. "You shouldn't feel lonely, kiddo. You got me!"

Katie smiled weakly. "Thanks. That means a lot."

"It should!" Molly giggled. "Who else would put up with your blubbering?"

Katie threw a handful of grass at her just as the bell rang. Time to go back inside and face the world. She grimaced. She'd be happier hiding out there for the rest of her life.

Molly must have noticed her hesitation. "Hey, if you don't let on that anything's the matter, Katie, no one will ever know the difference. They'll assume you're still on top of the world. And anyway, you are! There's a lot more to your life than just some guy."

Katie nodded thoughtfully as she stuck her arms into the sleeves of her jacket. "I'll just keep busy," she agreed. "That'll make me feel better. I'll work extra hard at my gymnastics, study like crazy for the chemistry test, put everything I've got into crew practice — " Katie stopped in her tracks and whirled around to stare at Molly with wide, horrified eyes. "Crew practice!" she repeated in a dazed tone. "I can't possibly go. I can't face him." She shook her head, determined. "I'll have to quit the team, that's all."

"That's all?" Molly echoed disbelievingly. "You'll quit and that's all? That doesn't sound like the Katie Crawford I know!"

Katie frowned. "What do you mean?"

"Just that the Katie I know — and she's somebody I admire a lot — never quits anything! She never does less than her absolute best. That's why she's a winner."

Katie took a deep breath. She turned to face the door leading back inside. "You're right. I can't quit. It's my team, too." She forced a smile for Molly's benefit. "I'll show Greg Montgomery. He might think he can toss me aside, but I'll show him that he's the loser in this deal!"

Molly swung the door open energetically. "All right! That's the spirit!"

But at the river that afternoon Katie realized that showing Greg was easier said than done. Crew practice was torture. After ten minutes her face ached from the false smile she'd pasted on it and her nerves were frazzled from the constant effort required to turn in the opposite direction every time she found Greg looking her way. She couldn't tell if he was even trying to catch her eye; she didn't give him a chance to. She figured she shouldn't have to — if he had something to say, he'd have all the opportunity anyone could

134

ask for during practice. After all, they usually spent the greater part of two hours in a boat together!

But not today. Pretty soon it was only too obvious to Katie that Greg was doing everything in his power to steer clear of her. He spent the first part of practice with the number two boat, and when he finally did turn his attention to the first boat, he blatantly ignored her. He split the rowers into two groups and put her in the other shell. Not a single word of criticism or encouragement was directed her way all afternoon, a real change from previous practices where she'd benefited from extensive private coaching.

Katie managed to keep a stiff upper lip until the end of practice, when Greg gathered the whole team on the dock for a few words about their upcoming race against New Devon on Wednesday. He had helpful hints for every single person there except her. As he wrapped up the pep talk and it became clear that he wasn't going to make even a token gesture to include her, she knew she had to do something drastic. She'd had coaches that she didn't get along with well before, but at least acted *professional*, and didn't let personal things get in the way of practice. And besides, what was going on with her and Greg was different. While the other guys dispersed to put away the equipment, she stormed up the dock to where Greg was standing, stomping her feet with as much force as her one hundred pounds could create.

Reaching him, she whipped the *Sally Ride II* yacht cap off her head and hurled it at his feet.

"I quit!" she shouted, stomping by him and on up the bank to the parking lot. She resisted the urge to look back over her shoulder to see if he was following her. By the time she got in and started her car it was very clear that he wasn't. She could see him out the car window as she backed out of her space. Not only hadn't he done anything to stop her, but he'd turned right back to the boathouse as if she'd been nothing more than a passing breeze. It was all the proof Katie needed — not that she needed any more than she had already — that he couldn't care less about her.

She drove home in tears, more certain than ever that she really had made a mistake about Greg. A terrible mistake.

Greg kicked his locker in the bottom left corner. Hard. It usually stuck so he had to do that every time he opened it anyway, but today it gave him a special pleasure. The locker flew open, rebounding with a clatter against the neighboring one, and he reached inside for his history notebook. Remembering that day just a few weeks ago, that first day Katie was going to be at crew practice, made him scowl. That day had crawled by, but it had been an enjoyable crawl, whereas this week time was dragging and every hour seemed more painful than the last. He had crew this afternoon — a race, even — but he wasn't looking forward to it at all. Katie wouldn't be there.

Greg dug through a stack of textbooks and pulled out *An Introduction to American History*, then slammed the locker shut. Now he was thinking about practice yesterday, the first time he saw Katie after their fight Monday night. He'd give anything to live the afternoon over — he wouldn't hide from her, he wouldn't let her quit and run away from him. "Live that day over!" he snorted to himself as he started down the hall through the crowd. Live Monday night over, rather. He'd explain everything and he'd do it right. Starting out by telling her how much he loved her. Boy, had he acted like a jerk.

He pushed the hair off his forehead impatiently and rounded the corner just in time to nearly run over Katie and Molly. His breath caught in his throat, and when he opened his mouth to say hello, only a croak emerged.

"Hi!" Katie said in a cool, breezy voice, meeting his eyes squarely and holding her chin high in the air as if she'd just dismounted from a balance beam. The expression on her face was self-assured and scornful.

Before Greg could croak out another syllable she'd marched on by with an impertinent flip of her ponytail. Even Molly didn't smile at him.

He was still gritting his teeth from the encounter as he took his seat in history. He couldn't tell if he felt more lonely or more mad. Lonely because Katie was right there, walking the same hallways he was, only he'd let her slip away. Mad because he knew he'd messed things up. He hadn't told Katie the whole story about seeing Chris, and now *she* was so mad at *him* he wouldn't have another chance to. And he was mad at his own stupid Montgomery pride which prevented him from approaching her to apologize.

137

Greg gave up trying to focus on Mr. Novato, much less listen to him. He started doodling on his notebook under where he'd written *Five Results of the Reconstruction*. He sketched a figure on top of a mountain — that was him. He'd just climbed it and maybe he'd ski down. At the foot of the mountain he drew a river. There was a little boat with a little Katie Crawford in it.

He stuck his pen behind his ear and slouched back in his chair to study the cartoon. He almost laughed out loud. That was him alright, never any place but on top, in any situation. That was where he always felt he had to be. Giving ground was not his nature. And nothing, he thought bitterly, not even Katie, could make him step down.

Chapter
13

Molly twirled a few strands of linguine onto her fork and looked across the kitchen table at her mother. "This sauce is fantastic, Mom! Maybe you should quit teaching and open a restaurant."

Mrs. Ramirez speared a piece of broccoli with her fork and shook her head at it disapprovingly. "The vegetables are a little bit soft. They just don't have produce here like they do in California."

"Oh, California." Molly drained her glass of milk and smiled at her mother. "You know, I don't even miss it much anymore."

"You have a milk mustache, honey," her mother pointed out. She smiled, too. "I don't really miss it, either. I'm happy with our little home here." She winked at Molly. "If only these Easterners would learn the difference between a kiwi and a pomegranate!"

Molly giggled. "It'll never happen!" She leaned one elbow on the table and concentrated on eating for a few minutes. She was kind of in a hurry because Katie was picking her up soon to go to an October Festival meeting at Jonathan's, but at the same time she was kind of in a mood to talk to her mother. She'd never gone into detail with her about what had happened at Ted's and her mom knew better than to ask. Molly always confided in her when she was ready to.

She looked at her watch unconsciously, and Mrs. Ramirez raised her eyebrows questioningly. "What's on the agenda tonight?"

Molly shrugged. "Katie's picking me up for a meeting. I won't be late."

"How's she doing, anyway? You told me she was having boy problems."

Molly laughed. "That's sure an understatement! Yeah, she said today she was ready to give up on the whole gender. I know how she feels."

Mrs. Ramirez tipped her head to one side and narrowed her blue eyes. "Has Ted really turned out to be such a villain?" she asked, her voice teasing. "I seem to remember it wasn't too long ago you thought he could just about walk on water!"

Molly crunched hard on a carrot slice. "Villainous isn't the word, Mom. I almost didn't know him, he was so unlike his old self." She sighed and pushed her plate away. "I just don't know what to think. He's still my boyfriend — I guess. But after last weekend it really seems like no boyfriend is better than one who's gone away to college."

"Maybe your expectations were too high," her mother suggested gently.

Molly shook her head decisively. "There's no excuse for the way he treated me."

"Do you think you'll give him another chance?"

Molly sighed even more deeply this time. "I don't know. I just don't know."

The phone rang as Mrs. Ramirez was standing up to take her plate to the sink. She answered it and then glanced at Molly. "Speak of the devil!" she mouthed.

Molly's heart sank and then leaped and then sank again. She jumped to her feet to sprint upstairs. "I'll get it in my room!" she called back over her shoulder.

Once in her small room, Molly perched uneasily on the edge of her bed, which was just a mattress and boxspring on the floor. She picked up the phone gingerly.

"Hello?" she said in a carefully precise voice.

"Molly, it's Ted," he said, his own tone hesitant. "Do you have a minute? I . . . I have something I really want to say to you."

"Actually, I'm on my way out," she answered, not offering any other explanation. Suddenly she felt her face grow warm with anger as she pictured Ted the last time she saw him, when he dropped her off at the train station after mumbling feeble excuses about having exams and the like. "Well, what do you have to say?" she added sharply. "Whatever it is, it's gotta be better than anything you had to say — or didn't — the other day."

"I know, Molly. That's why I'm calling. I feel bad. . . ."

"Why, isn't your studying going well?" Molly's laugh was sarcastic. "You certainly had enough time for it last weekend since I didn't hang around!"

"Molly, I really do want to — " Ted began earnestly.

Molly cut him off. "There's my ride. I'd better run. Good luck on your exams. See you!"

She slammed the phone down, breathing hard. *Of all the nerve!* she thought. That he could imagine she'd ever want to talk to him again after last weekend! She *didn't* want to talk to him . . . at least, not tonight.

Molly was still touching the phone when it rang again. She yanked her hand away as if the receiver had turned red hot. "Mom, would you get it?" she hollered. "And if it's . . . for me, tell him — tell whoever — that I left."

Knowing it was Ted on the other end, Molly listened to her mom say a few words before hanging up downstairs. As she pulled her jacket from the closet she almost laughed out loud. Not that the situation was humorous, but she was remembering what she'd said to Katie at lunch that day, that there was more to life than some guy, so she shouldn't let Greg get her down. One thing was for sure, Molly realized, it was easier to give good advice than it was to live it.

"Pretzel?" Jonathan Preston stopped in front of Katie and Molly, offering a basket of snacks.

The whole gang, or rather the October Festival committee, was gathered at his house for a planning session. Although, as Molly observed to Katie, they hadn't done much planning yet — they'd watched a movie on the VCR, pretty much cleaned out the Prestons' refrigerator, and that was about it.

Molly looked at Katie, waiting for a laugh or even a smile and got neither. "C'mon," she whispered, jabbing her friend with an elbow. "This is a party, not a funeral!"

Katie raised her eyebrows. "Look, I told you I didn't even want to come," she said. "You dragged me here, so you put up with me!"

They were sitting on a couch in the corner of Jonathan's den; Eric was talking with Jeremy, Elise, and Ben; Greg was just a few yards away laughing at something with Susan and Rich. "I guess you've got a reason to sulk," Molly admitted. "I should have let you stay home. Forgive me?"

"Sure." Katie took a sip from her soda and lowered her eyes back to her knees where she'd been staring all evening.

Just then Jonathan jumped onto an ottoman and waved for quiet. Everybody turned obediently to face him. "Time to get the ball rolling on this October Festival scheme, folks," he announced briskly. "Let's break up into small groups." He looked around and laughed. "I see we're *already* in small groups, so let's recombine according to who's working on what. How about . . . the concession stand subcommittee over there, and the entertainment advisors over there, and the people who are making arrangements for the visiting crew teams here — "

Molly turned to Katie. Her friend had gone pale. "I'm supposed to work with him," Katie whispered, shaking her long red hair. "What a joke!"

Before Molly could respond, Greg was speaking up. "That's okay, Jonathan," he said loudly. "I've already taken care of that. I've recruited the teams, and I can really do the rest of the stuff by myself."

Now Katie was beet red. Molly really thought she was going to explode, maybe leap to her feet and sprint out of the room, but she stayed put.

Jonathan pointed at Katie. If Greg had taken him by surprise he didn't show it. "That okay with you, Katie?" he asked.

She shrugged and nodded. "You bet."

"Great. Then you'll be redeployed to the. . . . Let's see." He peered down at his clipboard. "The Halloween-theme concession stands. And also don't forget your paper cups and plates! Okay. Now let's give the music committee something to work with. Any suggestions for a band?"

Everybody started talking at once, and Molly took advantage of the hullaballoo to talk in a low voice to Katie, who still looked shaken. "Gee, Katie, I'm sorry. That was pretty rotten of him, huh?"

Katie laughed but didn't look amused. "Right in character, I'd say!"

Molly tried to be diplomatic. "Well, I heard from Jonathan that the crew team lost in a big way today. Aaron told him Greg really chewed the team out afterward, too. Maybe that has something to do with his mood."

"Maybe," Katie said begrudgingly.

Molly reached down to retie the lace on one of her hot-pink hightop sneakers. "Doesn't sound like Greg, though, to yell at his team, do you think? I know he's a high-power guy, but I would have thought he'd be cooler than that."

"I really can't say." Katie took a handful of M&M's from a bowl on the end table. She tossed a red one in the air, tipped her head back and caught it in her mouth. "I don't know him as well as I thought I did, remember? Speaking of which, have you heard from Ted lately?"

Molly sighed. "Actually, he called tonight, but we didn't talk long. Basically, I hung up on him. I'm avoiding the issue, I guess. Maybe I just don't want to give him an opportunity to tell me to bug off!" She laughed lightly, with an effort. "If he really wants to talk to me, I suppose he'll keep trying."

"Hmm. Well, look." Katie slapped her hands on her knees purposefully. "I'm going to take off. Do you think you can get a ride home with somebody else?"

Molly glanced unconsciously at Eric and then nodded. "Sure." She gave Katie an encouraging, understanding smile. "It'll get easier, you know. You're handling it pretty well. See you tomorrow?"

"Yeah." Katie smiled. "If Jonathan wonders what happened to me, you can tell him his redeployed missile rocketed home early!"

Molly grinned. "For sure. G'night!"

"See ya."

Katie had hardly walked out the door when Eric joined Molly, who'd ducked into the kitchen to get a glass of water.

"Hey, stranger!" she exclaimed. As she greeted him with a warm smile she couldn't help thinking that it was too bad he hadn't approached her sooner. She knew Katie would have liked to talk to him, too, if only for a minute. Things were still pretty strained between them. "I haven't seen you in days, Eric. How's it going?"

"Can't complain, can't complain." He opened the fridge and bent over to peer inside, then pulled out a pitcher of orange juice. "I've missed seeing you around, though! When are we going to go out again?"

Molly stopped at the sink with her hand on the faucet. She'd been afraid this subject would come up. She filled her glass and turned around slowly, putting the smile back on her face. "Sometime soon," she said evasively.

Eric stepped toward her, icecube tray in hand. "One cube or two?"

She laughed. "Two, please!"

The ice cubes clinked into the glass. Eric dropped the tray on the counter and then placed his hands on Molly's shoulders. "Sometime?" he echoed with a teasing smile. "What about tomorrow night? I'm free."

Molly cleared her throat. "Actually, I have plans," she said. Then she saw the disappointment in Eric's eyes and ducked her head. "No," she admitted. "That's not true. I don't have plans."

"Then we're on?"

"Not exactly." Molly shrugged her shoulders under Eric's hands, then raised her own hands to take his and lower them to his sides. "Eric, I'm not busy tomorrow night but I'm . . . *busy*, you know?"

He shook his head, puzzled. "Try me again."

"Eric, you know what's happening with me and Ted?" Her voice was uncertain.

"I know, Moll, but this doesn't have anything to do with you and Ted."

"You're right, but that's not the point. The point is I'm . . . I'm disappointed because of Ted. I don't want to turn to someone else — even you — for that reason."

Eric leaned closer to her, his eyes warm, and she laughed softly. "I'll admit, it's tempting!" She raised a hand to his face and touched his cheek with one finger. "Very tempting. But Eric, any fun you and I could have together now would be kind of hollow. I can't expect you or anyone else to be a substitute for him. Do you know what I mean?"

Eric bent his head and kissed her lightly on the forehead. "Yeah, I do. And, Moll, thanks. Everybody should be as honest as you are."

Molly gave him a brisk hug and then winked. "We'll go to a movie or something, though. Sometime. Seriously!"

Eric gave her a thumb's-up sign as he left the kitchen. "I'll hold you to that, Ramirez!"

Molly watched him go and then turned back to the counter. The cubes left in the ice tray had started to melt around the edges so she dumped them in the sink and refilled the tray. She shook her head and smiled. Eric was really something. She liked him so much. But he was right about her being honest. If nothing else, she would always try to be that.

No, she couldn't substitute Eric for the real thing. Ted was still very much on her mind. And as Molly rejoined her friends she had a sinking feeling he would be for a long time.

Chapter 14

Katie stood on a tumbling mat in her backyard, with her left foot firmly planted on the ground and her right leg extended directly out in front of her. Slowly, leading with her chin, she curved her upper body backward, placed her hands, and then allowed her legs to follow, one at a time. A back walk over in the slowest motion she could manage. She slid right into a split and then froze that way, staring ahead of her at the lawn, entirely uninspired.

She was trying to come up with some new combinations to incorporate into her routines for the coming gymnastics season, but so far all she could think of were the same old things.

"Boring, boring, boring!" she complained out loud, bouncing up and off the mat. She reached impatiently for her tape player and punched the STOP button. The Bruce Springsteen song that had gotten her so fired up to work out in the weight room a few weeks ago only depressed her now by reminding her of Greg.

Katie took a deep breath. It was beautiful out! Almost like spring. The air was soft and fragrant, the sun was shining brightly through the pumpkin-orange leaves of the maple trees in the backyard, there was a gentle breeze . . . a day just made for roller-skating in Rosemont Park.

Five minutes later Katie was on her bike, pedaling down the driveway, her roller skates tied together by the laces and slung over the handle-bars. She felt like a bird let out of its cage. She threw her arms up in the air as she turned onto the street and rode with no hands for a few yards. No more work, I'm free! she felt like shouting. *Yippee*!

Gripping the handlebars again she lowered her head and started pumping for all she was worth. The wind in her hair felt good. It felt good to get out of her confining house and yard. A new atmosphere was what Katie needed.

She pedaled and pedaled, just enjoying the sensation, and then looked up to focus on a street sign as she passed. Harrison Avenue? she thought, surprised. Where am I going? This isn't the way to the park!

She kept pedaling and suddenly it hit her. She was on her way to Eric's house. Her bicycle just seemed to head there naturally. In the past she'd ridden this way a couple times a week when the weather was nice, to grab him to go skating or join a softball game or just to visit. She realized for the first time that she'd missed these rides, how special they had been.

150

She and Eric had had so many great times, too many to count, and they hadn't really spoken since the day they broke up. What a waste, Katie thought. What a waste of the friendship that started the whole thing off for them.

She turned onto Eric's street and considered riding past his house without stopping. No, she chided herself, don't be a wimp! Anyhow, maybe he won't even be home, she thought optimistically.

She leaned her bike against the Shrivers' mailbox and walked slowly up the driveway, hoping nobody was watching out a window. It felt funny — very funny — to be here. Katie knew Eric's house and yard as well as her own, but in a way she felt like a visitor to a foreign country. Everything looked familiar, but it was like looking at an old snapshot. It was some place she'd been a part of once but wasn't any longer.

Well, she thought, it's too late to run back to my bike now. I'm committed!

She pressed the doorbell and then stood shifting her weight nervously from one foot to the other. She was about to give up on anyone answering when the door swung open, and Eric peered at her through the screen.

"Katie!" To say he looked and sounded surprised would be putting it mildly. He smiled cautiously as if he wasn't sure if he should be happy to see her or not. He didn't add, "What are you doing here?" but the unspoken words hung in the air. She wasn't sure herself, but she hastened to break the ice.

"Um, I was just in the neighborhood," she explained, turning to wave casually in the direction of her bike. "I'm on my way to the park to go skating. Want to come along?"

Eric looked as if he were about to refuse, but then he nodded. "Sure. Why not? It's a great day for it." He opened the door and ushered her inside. "I've just gotta find my skates, okay? Be right back."

"Great!" After Eric left Katie glanced around the hallway, marveling at herself for being where she was, about to do what she was about to do. Roller-skating with her ex-boyfriend! Incredible! She should probably be amazed that he hadn't just slammed the door in her face.

But there they were, walking down the driveway together almost as if nothing had changed. Eric's manner was still guarded, though. As they mounted their bikes at the curb he tossed her a question. "Why did you really come over, Katie? I mean, no offense, but it's not like we've been on visiting terms lately."

Katie blushed and forced herself to meet Eric's eyes. The expression in them was carefully neutral. "Eric, I — it makes me sad that things are uncomfortable between us. I just want to be . . . friends."

The words sounded horribly cliché to Katie, but Eric must have detected the sincerity behind them. "I guess that's what I want, too," he said stiffly. Then his tone lightened somewhat. "Like I said, why not?"

They pushed off. Katie felt better as soon as they were riding. This way they didn't have to talk. By the time they reached the park her mood was almost bubbly. It was virtually impossible for her to feel any other way on such a sunny day.

They parked their bikes on the sidewalk by the fountain, which was turned off and dry as a bone. Katie sat down on the fountain's rim to lace her skates. Eric joined her. When they stood up to push off he wobbled a little and clutched instinctively at Katie's arm. They both burst out laughing.

"Remember that first time we went skating?" Katie asked with a broad smile.

Eric rolled his eyes and released her arm. Now he was gliding along smoothly. "How could I forget? I spent more time on my rear than anyplace else!"

Katie giggled. "You were really a sight, I'll say that." She skated up to him and then sprinted past. "Let's race!"

She held her lead around the fountain, but Eric caught her halfway down the road to the overlook. He hollered triumphantly as he whipped by and Katie waved her fist, laughing so hard she barely had the breath to skate. "I'll catch you, Shriver!" she called. "Don't be so cocky!"

She almost passed him when he slowed down, to execute a figure eight above the overlook, but he slipped by her again to head back the way they'd come. Katie took a deep breath and skated after him with all her might. As she gained on him slowly she thought how similar this scene was to so many in the past.

She drew abreast of him just as they reached the fountain and shouted, "I won!" They both skidded to a stop and collapsed on the sidewalk, panting and laughing. "Beat you, fair and square," Katie declared, lying back on the concrete with her hands behind her head.

"Naw, I let you win," Eric teased.

"You liar!" She gave him a gentle shove. "Admit it, I won."

"Yeah, you always win." Eric jumped to his feet and started skating around the fountain again. Katie sat up to watch him, reaching behind her to rebraid her hair. She'd only been kidding, but she probably shouldn't have said that. Even though Eric's voice had been light, it wasn't hard to tell she'd touched a nerve.

But he didn't look too bothered when he skated by her, one leg up in he air and his arms held over his head like a figure skater. Katie giggled. He did another lap and this time squatted low and kicked his feet out Russian-dancer style as he went by.

After the third lap he grabbed her arms and hauled her to her feet. "One more race?" he asked. "Or should we head straight for the sub shop?"

Katie didn't have to think twice. "Definitely the sub shop!"

By the time they'd biked there they were both starving. They walked in the door and headed for a table in the back. It wasn't crowded so they could take their pick. Katie found herself almost overcome by a weird déjà vu feeling. Had it really been that long since she'd come to the sub shop with Eric?

As soon as they sat down and dug into their

cheeseburgers, the haunted sensation left. Katie sank back against her chair, entirely relaxed. She asked Eric what he'd been up to, and he entertained her with his latest stories; when he asked about her life she did the same, carefully avoiding the subject of Greg. She couldn't tell if Eric knew about what had happened or not. If he did, he didn't let on. But she figured he must have heard something. The Kennedy gravepine was pretty thorough.

From current events they moved on to past history, reminiscing about the good times but not actually talking about their relationship. Katie laughed about the time Eric was pitching at the crowd's spring softball game and gave up a homerun to her because he underestimated Katie's strength as a hitter. They recalled parties they'd gone to together, bike rides and drives they'd taken, the night they'd gotten all dressed up and gone into D.C. to the theater and dinner at a fancy restaurant.

Katie smiled as Eric reminded her of the time they were lying in the hammock in her backyard and he chased her little brother up a tree after he pestered them one too many times, but her thoughts weren't on the story. She was simply absorbing Eric's face and voice, enjoying his company. A warm glow stole over her. If she didn't know better, she would have thought it was the old romance stirring inside her. With a start she realized that was exactly what it was. Suddenly she found herself wishing she and Eric had never broken up. She would have had this steady warmth to rely on always.

Eric slurped the last drop from his milk shake and then reached for an onion ring. "I'm glad you came by this afternoon," he said with a wink. "This is more fun than raking leaves!"

"It is fun," Katie agreed wholeheartedly. "It's nice to be with you again, Eric."

He frowned slightly, as if she'd broken some rule by saying that. "Yeah," he responded noncommittally.

"I've sort of missed this, haven't you?" she persisted, placing her elbows on the table and leaning forward with eager eyes.

"Missed this! You've got to be kidding." Eric shook his head disbelievingly. "What are you getting at?"

"Well, that . . . I don't know. That sometimes I wish — "

Eric held up a hand. "Stop right there," he said in a gruff voice. "Listen to yourself! I thought you just wanted to be friends."

"I do!" Katie said, flushing.

"Then why do you make it sound like you want to get back together or something?" he asked bluntly.

"I wasn't doing that!" Katie defended herself hotly. But she knew Eric was right. A few seconds ago there'd been something more than friendship showing in her eyes. She'd been inviting him to make some sort of move.

"Could have fooled me," Eric was saying. He picked the pickle off his burger and threw it back down on his plate. "Seeing you again, well. . . . All day you've been getting my hopes back up. You could have just left it at that." The pain and anger in his eyes made tears jump into her own. "What's going on, anyway? Things didn't work out with Greg so you're turning back to me?"

"No," Katie said quietly. "No!" she repeated, her voice rising. "It's not like that at all! Oh, I don't know what I'm doing." She started to cry.

Eric looked around them, embarrassed. A few people had glanced their way. "Katie," he said gently, "I'm sorry. Don't be upset." He leaned forward with a paper napkin to wipe the tears from her cheeks. "Now you're making me feel bad."

"Well, you should!" She sniffled. "You hurt my feelings."

"Did it ever occur to you that you were hurting mine?" he pointed out. Then he sighed, crumpling the napkin into a ball. "I am sorry, K.C. About everything. And I shouldn't have yelled at you. Forgive me?"

"Yeah." She laughed. "Will you forgive me?"

Eric paused. "Okay . . . if you give me the other half of your cheeseburger."

Katie smile weakly. "It's all yours."

Eric bit into the cheeseburger. "It may still hurt, Katie," he said through a mouthful. "Maybe it hurts you as much as it hurts me. But we can't go back to the way things used to be. As a couple we're over. Don't you think?"

"Yeah." Katie's eyes filled with tears again and she ducked to sip her milk shake to hide them. "Yeah, I guess we are."

"It's probably for the best."

"Probably."

They finished eating in silence. Finally Eric reached across the table to touch Katie's hand. "Let's go, kid."

Out on the sidewalk they stood by their bikes, looking at each other, both at a loss for words. "Hey, I'll ride you home," Katie offered, tipping her head to one side so her hair fell over her right eye.

Eric smiled. "Should we race?"

"In the streets of downtown Rose Hill?" Katie exclaimed. "Wait'll we get to the back roads!"

Eric was still smiling, but now his eyes became serious. "On second thought, Katie, let's not race. Let's just ride side by side."

"Okay." A slow grin spread over Katie's face. She nodded. "Side by side."

When they reached Eric's house, Katie tilted her bike by the curb, balancing herself with one foot on the street and one still on the pedal. Eric stopped next to her. "Thanks for a fun afternoon," she said. "Sorry I ruined things."

"No problem!" Eric said. "I mean, you didn't ruin anything. There was nothing to ruin. We're still friends." He put down his kickstand and walked around his bike to stand next to her. She put her arms around him and they hugged quickly. "I'll always love you, Eric," she whispered. "As a friend."

"Me, too," he whispered back. "So long."

"So long."

Katie felt more than a little sad as she biked home by herself in the twilight. For the first time since they broke up she really knew things were over for her and Eric, forever. In a way, though, she felt lighter at heart. The coldness between them had troubled her, and now the ice had melted. They might never be really close again, but they were friends.

And Greg? she thought as she pulled into her own driveway. He was another story altogether, and Katie still couldn't see the ending.

Chapter
15

"You're sure you don't want to come?" Katie asked Molly over the phone. "You mean to say the Rose Hill Mall isn't where you like to spend your Friday nights?"

It was the night before the October Festival Regatta and Katie still hadn't bought the decorations for the concession stands. The mall wasn't exactly where *she* wanted to spend Friday night, either, but she'd promised she'd take care of this, and she didn't want to let the others down.

Molly laughed. "It's really nice of you to ask me along, but I think I'll pass. Ted's fall break starts today and, well, I'm hoping he'll call me. I figure I'll give him a chance this time, unlike our last disastrous conversation. He might actually be home in Rose Hill right now!"

"Well, I can't blame you then," Katie conceded. "I hope he calls! And I'll see you in the morning. I'll be by at eight to pick you up, okay?"

"Happy shopping!"

Katie considered asking Will and Danny if they wanted to come along and play video games while she picked up her supplies but then abandoned the idea. They'd keep her there all night, and she really just wanted to get the errand over with. She threw her big denim jacket on and headed out to the garage.

Once in the mall, Katie made a beeline for the Hallmark store. In five minutes she was on her way out again with an enormous shopping bag filled with paper cups and plates, rolls of black and orange streamers, bunting, bags of confetti, and a Halloween monster mask. She hadn't had the heart lately to work on a genuine costume, although she knew a lot of her friends were creating masterpieces. The mask would have to do.

There was a chocolate chip cookie stand next to the Hallmark, and she stopped to buy a few for the road. Then the window display of a boutique a few doors down caught her eye. Katie strolled over and paused in front of it, longingly eyeing the gorgeous hunter green leather miniskirt and jacket on a red-haired mannequin. Katie sighed. She couldn't afford such an outfit in a million years. But the two-piece dress on the other mannequin was more in her league. She ducked inside.

Two steps into the boutique Katie stopped cold. Just a few yards in front of her a tall, blonde girl in a royal blue knit dress stood at the counter, carefully examining a paisley scarf she held at arm's length. The girl's back was to her but Katie

161

would recognize her anywhere. Chris Austin! What was she doing here?

Katie clutched her shopping bag tightly. It crackled loudly. She couldn't believe Chris was in town, much less in the very same store with her. She was home for the weekend to see Greg, that was it, Katie thought in disgust. She'd probably even have the nerve to come and cheer him on at the Regatta the next day!

Katie was still frozen at the entrance of the boutique, scowling, when Chris shook her head, handed the scarf back to the girl behind the counter, and turned to leave. The next thing Katie knew they were looking right at one another. For a moment she considered diving under a rack of dresses. She was really and truly trapped.

Chris had recognized Katie, and now she was actually approaching as if to speak with her. Katie held her ground, mortified. She didn't have anything to say to Chris, and she couldn't imagine Chris could have anything to say to her. Although, Katie thought suddenly, Chris probably didn't even know about Katie's brief romance with Greg. Why should she? Just play it cool, she counseled herself. Play it cool, and then get out of here. Fast!

Chris gave Katie a reserved but friendly smile. "Hi, Katie. How have you been?" she asked in her crisp, clear voice.

"Just fine, Chris. And you? How do you like college?" Katie was surprised that she could sound so casual.

"I just love it!" Chris raved. "It's such a challenge. I was just elected to the College Assembly so I'm busier than ever, but I like it that way."

"Congratulations!" Katie did her best to look impressed, although she would have been happier to hear that Chris had gotten kicked out of school. "It's great that you're keeping up your student government involvement."

"I couldn't give it up now," Chris admitted ruefully. "I'm hooked!" She nodded at Katie's armful. "It looks like you're having a pretty big Halloween party!"

Katie glanced down into her shopping bag and the monster mask looked back up at her. "Oh, this. This is for the October Festival tomorrow."

"The October Festival?" Chris pretended to be puzzled, or at least Katie assumed she was pretending. No doubt she'd heard all about it from Greg. She probably just didn't want to let on.

Katie explained the entire project, meanwhile wracking her brain for an excuse to bolt. When she stopped talking, Chris smiled, this time a little shyly. "Speaking of crew . . ." she began, and then paused. "How are things with you and Greg?"

Katie's jaw dropped, and she could feel the blood rush out of her face. She was stunned. If this was Chris' ideas of a joke, she was worse than Katie would ever have imagined her!

But before Katie had a chance to get mad, Chris was rattling on again. "It was really nice to run into him in Cambridge and hear that he's doing so well at school this year. He told me you'd joined crew — what fun! Anyway, I hope I get a chance to see him again this weekend. I just

163

came home for my stepmother's birthday." Chris was talking fast as if she were a little nervous. She didn't give Katie a chance to get a word in edgewise, which was probably just as well. Now she blushed slightly. "Katie, Greg told me that he was seeing you, and I'm really happy for you both. You don't have to worry that I'd hold a grudge or anything. Greg and I have gone our separate ways, and I wouldn't want it any other way," she concluded in a breathless rush.

Katie stared at her, speechless, and let go of her Hallmark bag. Bundles of streamers rolled all over the floor of the boutique. The two girls dropped to their hands and knees to retrieve them, bumping heads in the process. They both burst out laughing.

"I don't know why I was so nervous saying that," Chris confessed as she stood up and stuffed some streamers back into Katie's bag. "But you had such a funny look on your face, I had to say *something*. And then you got an even funnier look on your face!"

Katie shook her head. She was still in a daze, trying to grasp the significance of Chris's words. They wandered out of the boutique, and she collapsed on a bench flanked by potted palm trees. Chris sat down next to her. "Chris, I just can't tell you! You've totally thrown me for a loop."

"How come? Don't say I told you anything you didn't already know!"

"Actually, you did!" Katie laughed. She was so relieved that her encounter with Chris hadn't turned into a fist fight that she felt as light as a feather.

"You mean that it's okay with me that you're going out with Greg now?" Chris wondered. "Like I said, I don't have any hard feelings — "

"No, not that part!" Katie assured her. "It's the part about me going out with Greg. I thought *you* were going out with him!"

"Well, Katie, since I went to college things have been different. And actually there's a guy at Amherst, another school nearby — "

Katie cut her off again, wide-eyed. "You mean you and Greg didn't get back together when you saw each other at the Head of the Charles?"

"What on earth gave you *that* idea?" Chris exclaimed. She looked so flabbergasted Katie knew she couldn't be putting on an act.

"Oh, my gosh." Katie ran her hands through her hair and closed her eyes, her head swimming. Then she began giggling helplessly. "Oh, Chris. You'll never believe this." As best she could Katie explained to Chris about everything that had happened between her and Greg since he'd returned from his weekend in Boston. At the end Katie sighed deeply. "Well, maybe he just used you as an excuse to break up with me."

Chris let out a long, low whistle. She shook her silky blonde hair. "No kidding, Katie. Well, he could have fooled me. He talked a lot about you, and he sure *sounded* like he was head over heels in love with — wait a minute!" She held up a hand. As if I were going anywhere! Katie thought. "Maybe we're looking at this all wrong. Maybe that's not what he meant to do at all. Now what *exactly* did he say to you that night?"

Katie repeated the scene for Chris pretty much

165

word for word as well as she could remember it, and she realized for the first time that most of the words had come from her. Greg had only said that he'd seen Chris and that he couldn't get involved with Katie. He didn't get any further because she hadn't let him. The same thing had almost happened tonight with Chris. Katie had come pretty close to losing her cool, but Chris managed to squeeze her speech in first. If she hadn't, Katie would never have heard what Chris had to say. Maybe, she thought, just *maybe* I didn't get the full story from Greg two weeks ago.

"I'm sorry, Katie," Chris said sympathetically. "It must have been horrible. Do you know what I think? Stop me if I'm being too nosy."

"No, go on," Katie urged her. "Obviously I need all the help I can get!"

"I know Greg pretty well," Chris began. She smiled wryly. "After all, we went out for over a year. He can be pretty stubborn, in case you haven't noticed. He likes things his own way, and he has a lot of confidence they'll always turn out like that. But underneath it all, he's just like anybody else. He's vulnerable."

"He hides it pretty well," Katie observed.

"That's just his way," Chris said, her blue eyes serious. "He doesn't always want to admit that he has feelings and that they can be hurt. But from everything he told me in Boston, about how much he liked you and how much he thought you two were starting something special, I think he would have opened up to you the other night, if you'd given him the chance."

Chris's words were so matter-of-fact that Katie

couldn't be offended by them. She wasn't passing judgment, she was just helping Katie see something that should have been obvious to her a long time ago.

"You mean maybe his feelings for me hadn't changed?" Katie faltered, a catch in her voice.

Chris nodded. "I think he was just probably protecting himself the best way he knew how."

"Against what?" Katie was still mystified.

"Oh, I don't know. Against you. Against falling in love again and taking all the risks that come with it. You know, it was only a month ago when I came home for a weekend that he and I really talked about what's happened between us. Believe me, even though it's over, our break-up is still pretty fresh in both our minds."

Katie thought back to the scene outside the Bistro Français. Greg *had* tried to say something, if only she had listened. But it was too late now. She looked at Chris, her expression dismal. "I really blew it, huh?"

Chris laughed. "Don't give up so easily! I'm sure the damage isn't irreversible. Maybe it's up to you now to make a move. Show him love is worth the risk and that he's crazy to turn away from it."

Katie nodded thoughtfully. Chris was right. Her reputation for being fair and rational and all those other qualities Katie couldn't claim to possess was well-deserved. A smile slowly crept across her face. She hoped Chris was right. If she was lucky, maybe Greg did still care for her!

She pulled the bag of chocolate chip cookies from her shoulder bag and offered one to Chris.

"I owe you an apology, Chris," she said sheepishly. "I must have seemed so rude when we met just now."

Chris grinned. "I was trying too hard to be nice to notice!" They both laughed. They munched the cookies and then Chris glanced at the delicate gold watch on her slender wrist. "Ten minutes till the mall closes," she observed, getting to her feet. "Maybe I'll buy that scarf for Catherine after all. I'm certainly not going to find anything else tonight."

Katie rose also. "It was great bumping into you, Chris," she said, gathering up her decorations. "I can't thank you enough for setting me straight about Greg." She smiled slyly. "Now what's this about a guy at Amherst?"

"Oh, it's a little soon to say," Chris said. Her eyes sparkled. "But I have a feeling. . . . Let's just say he's absolutely the most wonderful guy in the world!"

The most wonderful guy in the world, Katie thought, waving good-bye to Chris as she headed back into the boutique. I guess that describes him pretty well. Greg Montgomery. The most wonderful guy in the world.

Suddenly Katie couldn't wait for tomorrow. She was actually looking forward to the October Festival Regatta she'd been dreading just an hour ago. Greg would be there. And she wasn't going to let a misunderstanding keep them apart.

Chapter
16

The next morning Katie woke up feeling like a new person. She sat up in bed and stretched luxuriously. She could see the brilliant blue sky through her bedroom curtains — the entire October Festival committee had prayed for good weather and it looked like their prayers had been answered.

She sprang out of bed, showered, dressed, gobbled some breakfast, and dumped the decorations in the back of her mom's Voyager. Then she scribbled a note to her parents, who were still asleep, and headed for Molly's.

Molly was ready, sitting on the front step of her apartment building. When she stood up and approached the car, Katie could see she was dressed as a tiger, with a black and orange striped rugby shirt, black tights and shorts, orange felt ears attached to a head band and whiskers painted across her face.

"Where's your costume?" she asked, looking doubtfully at Katie's sweats as she hopped in the car. Katie pointed to the mask in the backseat. "That's it?" Molly raised an eyebrow. "I'm disappointed, K.C.! Where's your creativity, your Halloween spirit?"

Katie braked for a Stop sign. "I haven't been in the costume-designing mood," she said. "Besides, I have something better on my mind this morning!"

She couldn't keep from grinning. Molly studied her suspiciously. "What's cooking in that head of yours?" she asked.

Katie tapped a lively tune on the steering wheel. It was all she could do to keep under the speed limit, she was so eager to get to the river. "Let me tell you what you missed by not going to the mall with me last night!" She described her conversation with Chris in detail, and Molly laughed until she had tears in her eyes.

"I wish I could have seen your face when she walked up to you!" Molly gasped. "I have to admit, I always thought Chris was kind of a cold fish, but it sounds like she's really not so bad. But, Katie, does this mean that things might not be over for you and Greg after all?"

Katie nodded, her ponytail bouncing. "I really hope so! Boy, do I hope so."

"Well, what are you going to do? What are you going to say to him?" Molly demanded.

Katie shrugged. She had an idea but she wasn't ready to share it yet, not even with Molly. She'd find out soon enough. "Oh," she just said, "I'll think of something when the time comes." She swung the car onto River Road, her pulse quickening. They were almost there! "By the way, Moll, did Ted call you last night?"

The smile faded from Molly's face, and she turned to the window with a sigh. "No. No phone call. No nothing. For all I know, he's not even coming home for his fall break. I guess there's nothing here for him anymore. He doesn't need me."

Molly was trying to hide it but Katie could tell she was deeply hurt. She tried to look at the bright side. "But, Molly, it's not like you guys have broken up or anything. Ted never said he didn't want to see you. Things are just — weird between you."

"Weird." Molly laughed grimly. "Is that what you call it when it turns out somebody you thought was in love with you couldn't care less about you? Oh, I'm sorry, Katie. Don't mind me. It's just so frustrating. Let's not talk about it." She reached up to adjust her tiger ears as Katie pulled into the parking lot above the boathouse. "Let's just get psyched for October Festival!"

The two girls jumped from the car, grabbed the decorations and headed down the bank. The air was filled with sound. Ben, Elise, Emily, and Scott were busily building concession booths by nailing wooden planks together; further down the river Jonathan was directing the construction of a makeshift band platform; Diana turned up the volume on Brian's new portable compact disk player as a hot Whitney Houston song came on.

Within minutes, Katie and Molly were both

caught up in the thick of things, laughing, chatting, draping streamers, helping newcomers unload their cars, and laughing at some of the Halloween costumes. Susan and Rich and a gang of their junior friends who were going to run the barbecue stand together were dressed as the characters from the board game "Clue." Susan, in a bright red satin sheath, was a slinky Miss Scarlet and Rich was Colonel Mustard complete with pipe. Diana and Jeremy were Laurel and Hardy, Fiona was Scheherazade from the *Arabian Nights*, although Katie thought she looked more like Barbara Eden in *I Dream of Jeannie*, and Jonathan was — who else — Indiana Jones.

"Some costume!" Katie teased him. "You wear that hat every day!"

"Yeah, but look at this!" Jonathan pointed to the rubber snake dangling from his belt on one side and the toy dagger on the other. "Tough stuff, huh?"

"I'm impressed!" Katie was helping Diana arrange homemade molasses cookies and lemon squares artistically on paper plates. A flash of morning sunlight on metal caught her eye and she looked up at the parking lot to see a van with "Maryville Crew Team" painted in blue on the side. She swallowed, both nervous and excited. Any minute now Greg and the Kennedy team would be arriving!

When Greg's car did pull in, she was the first to notice. From where she knelt, attaching orange and black bunting to the base of the band platform with a staple gun, she could watch him as he walked down the lawn to the boathouse. In a few minutes he and seven other rowers had one of the shells out of the boathouse and hanging in slings. Then they started carrying the long oars down to the shore.

Tons of people seemed to be arriving every minute. By ten o'clock the concession stands were ready and there were six crew teams warming up on the water. The crowd on the river bank was a dozen times bigger than the one the day Katie went to her first crew meet. Jonathan was jubilant. It was clear the October Festival was going to be a great success.

Katie had been keeping busy setting up even while she watched Greg carefully out of the corner of her eye. A few times he had looked her way, and once he'd even started up the bank toward her only to turn back. Somehow she felt closer to him than ever before. She could almost read his mind. She realized that all along he'd been as uncertain as she was, that he'd been sheltering himself behind his pride, too.

At ten-fifteen the Kennedy team assembled on the bank for a final pep talk before the race, which was scheduled to start at ten-thirty. Katie and Molly had just bought raffle tickets from Fiona; now Katie tucked her ticket in the pocket of her sweat shirt and pulled it over her head. She took off her sweat pants just as quickly.

Molly clapped her hands when she saw what Katie was wearing underneath. It was her crew uniform. "Go for it, K.C.!" she cheered.

Katie smiled and turned to walk down the hill to the river, rubbing her arm as she went. The breeze was cold on her bare arms and legs.

Greg saw her coming. When Katie was still twenty-five yards away she could see his eyes light up. They couldn't have been brighter than her own. He said something to the team and then left them in order to meet Katie at the top of the dock.

She'd been walking slowly but the last few steps she couldn't restrain herself any longer. She ran into Greg's arms. He hugged her so close she could barely breathe and when she protested he only squeezed her tighter.

"I can't believe you came back to me!" he whispered in her ear as he whirled her around. "I can't believe I'm really holding you again."

He placed her back down on her feet gently and kissed her on the cheek and then on the mouth. Katie started laughing. She couldn't help it, she was so happy. "Well, believe it, Monty," she said in a low, teasing voice. "I'm back for good! If you still have a place for me, that is."

She reached up to kiss him again. This time they were both distracted by a roar from the bank behind them. They turned in surprise to see that they were getting a standing ovation from the fans gathered to watch the crew races. Greg grinned and waved, and Katie blushed.

They only had a few minutes to talk alone before it would be time to start. They ducked behind the boathouse. "Here I can really kiss you!" Greg told her with a smile. "Having an audience cramps my style."

"I would never have guessed." Katie laughed and snuggled closer in his arms. It felt so good to be near him again.

"Well, it's true," Greg protested. "In reality I'm a shy guy!" He tugged at her ponytail. "So, what made you do it, Katie? Why are you forgiving me for being such a jerk?"

Katie shook her head. "No, I was the jerk, not you. I should have given you a chance to tell me. . . . What *were* you going to tell me?"

"It's a long story. We don't have time now. Let's just say I'm glad you didn't give up on me." He kissed her on the nose.

"I couldn't give up on you," Katie declared. "I finally knew I couldn't quit, on you or on crew. So here I am!"

Just then they heard a whistle. Greg grabbed Katie's hand. "Let's go!"

The temporary coxswain of Kennedy's first team was happy to give up his place to Katie, and she settled in the boat, the familiar rush of adrenaline making her toes and fingers tingle. They rowed toward the starting line and Katie leaned forward slightly. Greg caught her eye, mouthed the words "I love you," and winked. The race was on!

Katie had rarely been so intent on anything as she was now on the powerful strokes of the eight rowers she was directing. She could tell that Greg was rowing like he'd never rowed before. When they reached the finish she could see their five opponents in her peripheral vision — two boats on the left of her, three on the right — and she could hear the crowd cheering. Her boat was ahead! They'd won.

Things got wild on the shore after the races were over. The concession stands sold out of their edibles, people danced like crazy to the funky D.C. band Brian and Karen had hired, Jonathan judged a zany Halloween costume contest. During one of the band's breaks, Fiona waved the crowd to silence to announce the winner of the raffle.

"Are you ready?" she called. Everyone cheered. "All right! The lucky person holding the ticket with this number on it wins a private cruise for two with Captain Greg Montgomery on his sailboat, *Sally Ride II*." She paused dramatically. "And remember, the proceeds from the raffle will be used to buy new racing tanks for the crew team. Thanks for your support!" She paused again.

"Get on with it, Stone!" Jonathan yelled.

Fiona laughed. "Okay, okay. The winner is. . . ."

Katie pulled the raffle ticket out of her sweat shirt pocket with her left hand. Her right was holding Greg's.

". . . Number 1172!"

Katie glanced down carelessly at her ticket, then looked again. "Hey! That's me!" she started to shout. But before she could run up to Fiona with her ticket, Greg had taken her in his arms.

He whispered something in her ear and she nodded. She wasn't even aware of Fiona drawing another number — she was too busy kissing Greg. She didn't need to turn in her ticket. She was already the winner.

"Chili dog?"

Molly had been standing on her tiptoes, peering over Ben Forrest's shoulder to see who won

176

the raffle. Now she whirled around, the familiar voice making her heart jump. Ted stood behind her with a hot dog in each hand, a sheepish smile on his face, and a T-shirt reading PLEASE FORGIVE ME on his chest.

Molly burst out laughing. "Ted!" she exclaimed, moving to hug him, chili dogs and all. Then she remembered she was supposed to be mad at him and stopped in her tracks. "What are you doing here?" she asked in a cooler voice.

"Looking for you!" He gestured with a hot dog at the crowd. "It took me half an hour to find you. This is a madhouse! Here, take one of these things before I shower somebody with chili."

Molly took a chili dog but continued to stand her ground. Ted's eyes were so warm, though, and he seemed so happy to see her, it was hard to resist succumbing to his mood. But there were still a lot of things he had to explain.

"Molly," he said, waving his now-free hand in front of her eyes. "Lighten up! I thought this was a party."

"Oh, it is," she acknowledged.

"Aren't you having fun?" he asked, biting into his chili dog.

"I *was*," Molly said with emphasis.

"Wait a minute." Ted finished his chili dog and then studied her, puzzled. "Meaning it stopped being fun when I showed up?" He grabbed her around the waist and brought his face close to hers. "I thought we'd both been looking forward to this for weeks." He grinned and tried to kiss her.

Molly dropped her chili dog on the grass so she could use both hands to push him away, but he wouldn't release her. "You're right. I've been looking forward to it for weeks! Looking forward to your fall break when it would be *convenient* for you to spend some time with me."

"Molly, be fair!" Ted exclaimed. "I had exams. You have to understand, I've been thinking about you as much as ever, maybe even more, but I've just been busy."

"Too busy to even be polite to me when I came out to surprise you?" Angry tears sprang to Molly's eyes. "Too busy to notice that you forced me into making up excuses to leave early?"

Ted bowed his head, his forehead wrinkling. "I'm sorry about that," he said in a low voice. "I was incredibly selfish. I know I hurt your feelings." He put a finger under her chin and raised her face so their eyes met. "I am sorry. That's what I tried to tell you the other day when I called. I've tried a few times since then, actually. You never seem to be home." He smiled crookedly. "I'm trying again. That's what the stupid T-shirt is for."

Molly couldn't help giggling. "It is pretty stupid. But thanks."

Ted put his arm around her and held her tightly. This time she didn't resist him. "You *have* forgiven me, haven't you?"

Molly smiled to herself, her cheek pressed against Ted's chest. She didn't have a choice. "Of course," she said softly. "I would have, even *without* the T-shirt."

Ted laughed. "That's my girl!" He took her

small hand in his bigger one and led her apart from the October Festival crowd. They sat under a tree where they could still hear the music and see the action but also have some privacy.

Ted spread his jacket on the grass and lay back, pulling Molly down beside him. "I can't wait to be alone with you," he whispered huskily.

"We are alone," Molly pointed out.

"Really alone," Ted revised.

She smiled. "Me, too."

He put his arms around her and this time she let him kiss her. It was a long time before their lips parted and when they did their eyes remained locked. "I love you, Molly," Ted said simply. "Since I went to school a lot of things have changed for me. The world seems a lot bigger and scarier. But one thing's never going to change and that's what I feel for you."

"Oh, Ted," Molly said, a catch in her voice. "It makes me so happy to hear you say that. I was afraid — I was afraid you were leaving me behind."

"No way." He tickled her nose with a blade of grass. "How could I leave you when you're the best thing that's ever happened to me?"

"What about Sarah?"

"Sarah?" he echoed blankly.

"Sarah!" Molly exclaimed with a scowl. "Your *friend* downstairs from English class. The one with the long blonde hair."

"Long blonde hair?" He tipped his head to one side, looking confused.

"Long blonde hair!" Molly repeated emphatically. "Are you deaf?"

"Well, first of all Sarah, my *friend* downstairs, has brown hair. It's long but it's definitely brown. Secondly she *is* just a friend. What does she have to do with you and me?"

"Don't you like her?" Molly persisted.

"Of course I like her! But that's it. She's just a nice kid."

"You mean it wasn't her you called on the phone when I was in the bedroom changing? You weren't breaking a date?"

Ted had to think for a moment. "When you were changing?" Then his eyes lit up. "Yeah, I did have a date." He laughed. "With my roommate, Kent! I was calling him at a friend's room. We were going to meet for a pizza study break. I didn't want to tell you I had other plans, because I didn't want to hurt your feelings."

"Oh." Molly considered this and then raised one finger triumphantly. "What about that *other* girl then, the blonde one who talked to you outside the locker room after the game that day?"

"Her?" Ted rolled over on his back and laughed. "She's the resident counselor down on the girls' floor. She goes out with the R.C. on my floor! Ha-ha!"

Molly frowned. "What's so funny?"

"You! I can't believe you're jealous of *them*. Neither of them could hold a candle to you, Moll. None of the girls in school could."

"They couldn't?" Molly's eyes were wide.

"Nope. None of 'em."

"Yeah, but" — Molly rested her elbows on Ted's chest and looked down at him — "but they're there and I'm here. I'm at a disadvantage."

Ted shook his head. "You're only at a disadvantage if you feel like you are. As long as you trust me and believe in me everything will be okay," he said with conviction.

Molly remembered the hurt she'd felt when she'd stepped into Ted's new world and he'd rejected her. Now that they were together again that seemed like a hundred years ago, but she couldn't forget it, even if she wanted to. "It was hard to believe that you cared for me when I wanted to be close to you and you didn't let me. It was hard not to feel at a disadvantage when you made me feel out of place visiting you," she said sadly.

A shadow crossed Ted's face. "I'm sorry, Molly. That was so wrong of me. No matter how much work I had I should never have treated you that way. I'm still learning how to handle my life there. Will you be patient with me?"

"I'll be anything if it means we can stay together," she assured him, her eyes glowing. "I guess maybe we both have to work a little harder at it, huh? I mean, now that we're living in two different worlds."

"I'll try if you'll try," Ted said. "I think we can do it. I think we can do anything."

A sudden breeze sent a shower of golden leaves down on them just as they kissed. "I love you so much, Ted," Molly said. She meant it more than she'd meant anything in her life.

"I love you, too, Molly. Whiskers, tiger ears, and all."

Chapter 17

The first day of November was as warm as summer. "Perfect for the last sail of the season!" Greg said to Katie with a happy smile.

They'd made the drive to the Fillmore Nature Preserve in the hill country of western Maryland in just under two hours, towing the *Sally Ride II* behind the white Mercedes. By noon they were on the water and running before a light, steady breeze.

Greg wouldn't let Katie touch a single rope. "No, ma'am," he said firmly. "You're the guest of honor on this cruise, remember? You won the raffle, so today I'm yours to command!"

"Then how come you're the one giving *me* orders?" Katie teased.

"Was I?" Greg laughed. "Sorry! I guess I can't help playing captain when I'm on the deck of this baby. Isn't she beautiful?"

Katie nodded. "Sure beats rowing, huh?"

She was perfectly happy to sit back in the stern of the boat and let Greg do all the work. It was fun to watch him. His expression was intense, but happy at the same time. He was clearly in his element. And she felt pretty good right now, too. She swept the hair off her neck and pinned it up with a barrette, then unbuttoned one more button at the neck of the shirt she was wearing under her V-neck sweater. Maybe she'd get a tiny little tan today.

She tilted her head back, sighing deeply in contentment. It was hard to believe that just a couple days ago she'd been so weighed down with concerns. Today she felt as light as the hawk she could see soaring above the pine trees circling the lake, as light as a falling leaf caught in an upswell of wind.

Katie closed her eyes and let the sun warm her face. She started thinking about last night. After the October Festival, she and Greg had bypassed a party at Jeremy's and Fiona's house to go out to dinner by themselves and then for a drive. She smiled to herself and then jumped. Greg had placed a hand on the railing on either side of her head and was blocking her sun.

"I like that look on your face," he said, his blue-green eyes crinkling at the corners. "What are you thinking about?"

"Guess!" Katie's lips curved in a smile.

"Not about last night." They both laughed. "Well, that *is* funny," Greg observed before he kissed her. "I was thinking about the exact same thing."

Katie's eyes popped open in midkiss. "Isn't the

boat going to crash or something if you don't watch it?" she asked nervously.

"Oh, yeah!" Greg looked around, pretending to panic. "We're out of control! Help!"

Katie punched his arm playfully. "Okay, I'm stupid! I don't know how boats work."

"It's easy." Greg settled next to her on the seat. "It's a nice big lake, and with a breeze like this we can settle into a tack and then sit back and relax." He put his arm around her and gave her shoulder a squeeze. "Think you can get the hang of it?"

"With you here to coach me, I'm sure I will."

"That reminds me." He leaned forward and reached behind him to pull something out of his back pocket. When he unfolded it, Katie saw it was the hat he'd given her for good luck, the one she threw at him the day she quit the crew team. Now he placed it gently on her head. "Will you come back on the crew of the *Sally Ride II*?" he asked, his eyes serious.

"Back on the crew?" Katie raised her eyebrows. "Who are the other members?"

"You and nobody else! Well, there's also me. Just the two of us."

"That sounds kind of nice," Katie said thoughtfully, her eyes mischievous.

"It will be." Greg wrapped his arms around her. "Thanks, Katie," he said, his voice muffled in her hair. "Thanks for giving me another chance."

She lifted her face to his. "I figured we both deserved one. And I'm so happy now! But Greg. . . ." She hesitated. "How can I — can *we* — be sure that what . . . happened . . . before doesn't happen again?"

Greg hugged Katie tightly and then released her to take the tiller before answering. "It won't happen again," he said with certainty. "I made a mistake, Katie, and now I can admit it." He looked at her with a wry grin. "And believe me, that's not the easiest thing in the world for me to do!"

"I know." Katie smiled and adjusted her cap. "So what was your mistake?" she asked in a soft voice.

"I was afraid to get involved with you. Afraid that you might turn out to be another Chris," he said honestly. "Someone who would just pass through my life. My mistake was doubting whether loving you could be worth the pain that might come after, if the same thing happened to us when you graduated that happened with her."

Katie watched him as he spoke. She could see a faint flush steal under the tan along his cheekbones. This was obviously hard for him to say.

She reached up and kissed him on the ear, then flashed him a silly smile. "I'm glad you're talking to me about this. But Greg, I'm not Chris! That wouldn't be such a bad thing to be, though." She smiled, thinking about her half hour with Chris at the mall. She hadn't mentioned it to Greg and she didn't plan to. It was something that was better kept to herself. "You and I have something new," she continued, becoming serious. "What happened in the past — to both of us — well, we can't let it get in the way of the future."

"I know. Now that I'm with you I realize how

stupid I was. I love you, Katie." He gave her a quick kiss and then quickly sat up. "Get ready to come about!"

After he'd swung the boat around he slid back in next to her, his broad shoulder brushing hers. He turned to her and looked in her eyes for a long time before speaking again. "I love you more than I ever thought I could love anyone."

Katie tucked her left foot under her and rested her chin on her knee. She fidgeted with the lace on her moccasin. "But what about Chris?" she asked.

Greg put a hand gently on either side of her face and made her look at him. "Chris was special to me," he said. "I can't deny that. But she was . . . I don't know. In a way she was so much like me that sometimes being with her was like looking in a mirror, you know? You — you're different. I mean, you and I have a lot in common, but you fill in the empty places in me, too." He laughed and ran his hands through her hair to rest them on her shoulders. "Does that sound stupid?"

Katie smiled and leaned against him. "Not at all," she said softly. "That's exactly the way *I* feel about *you*."

"Hey, how do you like that?" Greg shouted, grabbing the cap off her head tossing it aside. "Yahoo!" He pulled her so close he nearly let go of the sail. "Let's say we really go for a sail someday, Katie," he said eagerly. "All around the world!"

Katie just smiled. She had a feeling she and Greg were already sailing together into the most wonderful experience of their lives.

Coming soon . . .
Couples #27
SWEET AND SOUR

"You really are incredible when it comes to dealing with kids," Justin McMaster said, shaking his head in amazement as he and Elise stepped out into the hall of the Rose Hill Children's Hospital.

"Thanks." Elise turned to look at him more closely. He wore a green hospital jacket over a faded blue T-shirt and a pair of old Levi's with a patch on one knee. He was tall, but not as tall as Ben, and when he smiled his whole face lit up. His eyes, however, remained solemn.

Justin looked her in the eye. "You know, you really should think about volunteering at the hospital — like me."

Elise felt nervous and happy at the same time. It was partially because of what Justin had just said, and partially because of the way he was looking at her. "I already have volunteered," she admitted. "In fact, I was on my way to the supply room to get my uniform when I saw the little girl crying."

"No kidding! That's great!" His eyes continued to hold hers, causing Elise's heart to skip a beat. She didn't know why, but she was suddenly very conscious of his handsome, broad shoulders beneath the hospital jacket, and the tilt of his mouth as it curved into a broad smile. Looking at him made her feel spacy and lightheaded, and she leaned against the wall.

"What do you say we make rounds together?" Justin placed a hand on the wall above her head. "It'll be more fun that way."

Elise looked at Justin. He was smiling at her — a nice, warm smile that Elise was getting more and more accustomed to.

"You're on," she said, almost in a whisper.